I0690555

SWIM MOVE

Books by David Chill

Post Pattern

Fade Route

Bubble Screen

Safety Valve

Corner Blitz

Nickel Package

Double Pass

Tampa Two

Flea Flicker

Swim Move

Hard Count

Curse Of The Afflicted

SWIM MOVE

A Novel By

David Chill

Copyright © 2019 by David Chill

All Rights Reserved

This book is a work of fiction. Names characters, places and events are products of the author's imagination and are used fictitiously. Any resemblance to actual events, locations or persons living or deceased, is purely coincidental. The author assumes no responsibility for errors, inaccuracies, omissions, or any inconsistency herein.

"Children begin by loving their parents. After a time they judge them; occasionally they forgive them."
--Oscar Wilde

Swim Move

One

It is an unfortunate truth that children often pay the price for the sins of their fathers. In the case of Amanda Zeal, however, she seemed to have lived a dreamy life for the better part of her twenty-four years. But looks are deceiving, and Amanda had committed a few costly sins of her own during that stretch.

I had played football with Amanda's father back in high school, and we had not bothered to stay in touch. That was fine by me. Her father, Phil Zellis, was a tenacious guy who never shied away from a fight. In fact, he would instigate many of these, often taking curious steps to provoke physical altercations. It didn't matter if the other kid was bigger or smaller than he was. What mattered to Phil was being able to dominate anyone in his path. He called it getting respect. The school psychologist called it something else.

It had been a few decades since I had last seen Phil, and like most of us who landed in middle age, he looked quite different as an adult than he did in high school. But Phil's changes were largely cosmetic. When he entered my office, he was wearing a black leather waistcoat over a navy blue cashmere sweater, and had on tailored gray slacks. He sported a shiny gold Rolex, and his tan loafers had tassels on them. Even the haircut seemed expensive. From a distance, he probably appeared dapper and elegant and handsome. Up close, however, he looked like none of those things. His physique was sturdy and tough, and he didn't come across as someone to be taken lightly. His face conveyed a hoodlum-like quality, albeit a hood who had managed to acquire an awful lot of money.

Amanda walked into my office behind him. She had an athlete's physique, square shoulders and long arms, and she was as attractive as he was repulsive. Her demeanor was confident and poised. She had long blonde hair and a pretty face, accented with soft-violet eye shadow and deep-red lipstick. She was dressed in a tight black top and tight black pants. They looked nice on her. Everything looked nice on her. I started to wonder if the two of them were actually related.

"Burnside," he said, reaching out to shake my hand. "It's been a while. You look good."

"I know."

The slightest hint of an ugly smile appeared quickly in the corner of his mouth. It disappeared just as fast. Amanda just gave me a bored look and didn't say anything. They sat down.

"You were probably surprised by my call this morning," he said.

"Not much surprises me these days," I said slowly. "But I don't expect much, either."

Phil took this in. "I should have kept in touch. But you know, life gets in the way."

"I'd say life's been good to you," I observed.

"Good and bad," he said. "Like everyone else, I guess."

For Phil, it was probably more good than bad. "So, what have you been doing the last twenty-five years?" I asked.

"I'll give you the short version. Got married early. Suzy was my college sweetheart. We were married junior year."

"Let me guess. She was pregnant."

Amanda stopped looking bored and Phil shot me a suspicious glance. "How did you know?"

"Deductive reasoning," I smiled, wondering if he would understand I was lying. But Phil's story was not all that unusual. I had a few teammates at USC whose girlfriends ended up pregnant. Some players went and married them, but most of these couples ended up divorcing within a few years and moved on. Except for the kids, though, whose lives were forever shaken by their parents' split. When it came to girls, I made sure I took precautions, the careful approach of someone who had lost both of his parents before his eighteenth birthday. When life throws you curveballs, you become tentative about what else the world has in store for you.

"You're right," he admitted. "We got married, we had Amanda. Our next kid, Aaron, we waited five years for him. At least I had a paycheck by then. Working in Suzy's family business."

"Good job security," I remarked.

"Best kind there is."

"And now you're divorced."

The look Phil shot me this time was less suspicious and more annoyed. "You figured that out, too?"

I smiled and shook my head. Before Phil came over, I took some time and combed through the internet. Even though Phil and I both grew up in Culver City, his journey was far different from mine. We had played football together, but while I managed to secure a scholarship to USC, Phil went to Vassar College in upstate New York, a pricey school that had no football team, and to my knowledge, did not give scholarships to C+ students. Phil was the type of kid who was bright but never applied himself. There was something inside of him that was troubled. His parents, mostly his father, managed to lift him out of whatever adverse situation he got himself into. I had no idea if Phil ever worked through his demons. Most people did not.

"No," I said. "After you called, I got curious, so I did a background check on you. Some things are matters of public record."

"Like marriages and divorces."

"Right," I said, not bothering to add property values were also readily accessible. The son of a policeman, Phil had come a long way from Culver City to Beverly Hills, from a modest house off of Jefferson Boulevard to a twelve-million-dollar mansion north of Sunset. I didn't enter those subtle details into our conversation. Some things did not need to be said. At least not right away.

"You married?" Phil asked.

"Yes."

"Kids?"

"One. We're looking at schools now for the fall."

"Colleges?"

"Kindergarten. He just turned five."

"Wow," Phil said, leaning back. "You started late. My daughter's almost twenty-five. My son's nineteen, he just entered USC last year."

"Good school," I said approvingly and turned to Amanda. "By the way, I've seen you on TV a lot the past few months. College football games. I guess you shortened your name to Amanda Zeal. Was Zellis too hard for the play-by-play guys to pronounce?"

That finally got Amanda to look slightly amused. "No. But it's not uncommon for people in the media to change their names. Have one that's catchy. Seems to be working for me. I'm trying to move up to NFL games soon."

It didn't hurt that she was very attractive, I thought, although being pretty was only part of the job of a sideline reporter. On air, Amanda came off as savvy and confident, and she seemed enthused with what she was doing. In person, it was another story.

"You used to be a football coach at SC," she said. "Too bad you left before I started. I could have interviewed you at halftime."

I looked past her at the blank wall on the other side of my office. I really should hang some pictures. I thought about what she said. In my brief tenure as a football coach, I avoided the media like the plague, and let our head coach,

Johnny Cleary, talk with them. I was blessed with the innate ability to make an inflammatory comment at just the wrong time. The last thing I wanted was a camera documenting that.

"Interviews are for head coaches," I said. "That's one of the things they do well. Talk without really saying anything. But I'm sure a lot of them are happy to speak with a pretty girl, even if she's in front of a TV camera."

"Yeah, pretty," Phil muttered. "That may be part of her problem."

"Dad ... "

"Look, Amanda, that really is part of your problem. That's always been part of your problem."

She glared at him and turned away. I turned back to Phil.

"Is that the reason you're here?" I asked curiously, wondering if a psychotherapist might have been a better choice for them.

Phil nodded. "Amanda's been a magnet for guys since she was twelve years old. Remember the Moose? I had Moose go and have some conversations with a few of them," he said, rubbing his knuckles and giving me a knowing nod. Moose was an unsavory character from our high school days. Even though Phil Zellis had become a Beverly Hills denizen, it was clear he obviously hadn't left his working-class roots behind.

"Good Lord, are we going into this now?" Amanda sighed, exasperated.

"Old habits die hard," I pointed out.

"Well," said Phil, "I admit I got into my share of scrapes as a kid."

"Probably more than your share," I clarified.

He nodded again. "My dad taught me how to fight. And to never back down from a fight."

"If I recall, you provoked an awful lot of them."

He shook his head. "No. It was always someone else. Kid cutting in front of me in line. Someone not looking where they were going and banging into me. Not apologizing. Not showing respect. I didn't start any of those fights. But I sure finished most of them."

I remembered that well. "That's why your dad had you go out for football. Good place to get your aggressions out."

Phil looked me square in the eye. "You psychoanalyzing me?"

"Sort of," I said. Football was one of the few places where a guy could physically manhandle someone, lift them up and slam them to the ground, without any fear of criminal charges being brought. In fact, when done at a propitious moment, they would often get showered with applause. In any other setting, they would be looking at jail time. On the football field, they'd be more likely to get a trophy. It was a game that attracted all sorts, some who were well-adjusted, others who were borderline psychopaths.

"And if I recall, you got into a few brawls yourself, Burnside."

I didn't disagree. Instead, I decided to redirect the conversation. "Tell me more about your daughter's situation."

Phil Zellis paused for a moment. "So, Amanda's had plenty of boyfriends. Maybe too many. I don't like the latest one."

"You don't like any of them," she snarled.

"He's your dad," I said. "He's not supposed to like your boyfriends."

Phil glared at me. "Maybe you should lay off the wisecracks."

"Sure," I said.

"Take a good look at my daughter. She's got a shiner. Covers it up well with makeup, but you can see it if you look hard enough. Her boyfriend, Wyatt, he had some bruises on his face."

I looked hard. I didn't see much. "This Wyatt have a last name?"

"Angstrom," he replied with a sneer.

I turned to Amanda. "So, what happened?"

"I fell down."

I turned back to Phil. "You think this Wyatt hit her?"

"I don't know. She said they were attacked on the street. And she fought back," he responded, a measure of pride forming in his voice. "Probably better than he did."

I looked over at Amanda. She was gazing out the window. I turned back to Phil.

"Tell me more," I said.

Phil gave a small smile. "I had given her some pepper spray for protection. That ended whatever dispute those punks had. Amanda and her boyfriend were able to make it back to her apartment okay. Well, not exactly okay. But she took care of the situation. Her boyfriend supposedly owns a gun, but she told me he didn't have it on him last night. Might have saved him from getting beaten up."

"Interesting. You teach your daughter how to fight?" I asked, noticing Amanda had balled her right hand into a fist and the knuckles were starting to turn white.

"Sure, I taught her to defend herself. But she usually didn't need to. I got her into sports early on. Swimming, soccer, basketball, karate. Girls who play sports are just more confident. That's what makes this episode so unusual. She said these guys pulled up in a van and attacked them. No idea why."

"This true?" I asked her.

"If he says so."

Phil's eyes narrowed and he studied her for a moment. "Baby, would you mind waiting outside? It'll just be a couple minutes."

"With pleasure," she said, pulling out her phone as she walked out. She closed the door hard enough for us to notice, but not so much that it slammed.

"Amanda doesn't seem to want to be here," I noted. "Or want any help from me. If she was attacked, it might have been random and it might not have. Probably not, is my guess. But if she's not willing to cooperate, it'll make any investigation I do more difficult."

"She doesn't want the publicity," Phil said. "Thinks it'll affect her job. I'm more concerned with her safety. I told her I was pulling rank. I need some answers. I don't want this to happen again."

"Okay. Let me ask you something personal. And I'm not trying to psychoanalyze your family. Just trying to learn more. Your daughter have any problems growing up?"

I waited for Phil to shoot me another look, but it didn't happen. Instead, he considered this for a moment. "She was a little rebellious as a teenager. Tested limits. I guess we all did. Maybe she more than most. The divorce and all. Probably harder on her than us. I don't think she ever really forgave me or Suzy."

"Okay," I said. "What would you like me to do here? Find out what happened?"

"Uh-huh."

"Did Amanda and Wyatt file a police report?"

"They did. For what it's worth."

"Where did they say it happened?"

"Beverly Hills. On their way home, walking back from dinner."

"She still live with you?"

"Nah. I told her she could, but you know. Wants her independence. She has an apartment a few blocks south of Wilshire. Just off Beverly Drive."

"Where were they going to dinner?"

"Some sushi bar," Phil peered at me. "Why does that matter?"

I peered back. "Sometimes it matters, sometimes it doesn't. The more I know, the more I can help you."

"Oh, like in *Jerry McGuire*. Help me to help you."

I nodded and didn't say anything. The quote originally came from an old cop movie called *Prince Of The City*. But there was nothing to gain by correcting a wealthy client over a trivial matter.

"Look," he said, "I should also tell you that I hired the Moose again to look after her. Provide some security and all. Amanda wasn't crazy about that, what with her going out with this Wyatt guy and all. But I told her, baby, the President of the United States has a team shadowing him.

You're in the limelight now. Get used to it."

I thought back to high school. The Moose was Anthony Machado, a teammate on the football team, a 6'6" monster who could intimidate people with just an angry glare. The assets Moose brought were clearly brawn over brains. His grades were so bad that he barely graduated from high school. He didn't get any scholarship offers, and his parents did not have the financial wherewithal to pay for college. While he did receive financial aid to play at a junior college in Oklahoma, he flunked out after one year. Even the most accommodating of colleges still had a few academic standards, with reading and writing a basic requirement for matriculation.

"You kept in touch with Moose after all these years," I remarked.

"I've hired him here and there. He can be useful. Moose isn't the sharpest tool in the shed, but he has some, well, presence. And he could use the money. He's had a rough life."

I frowned. "Just what kind of business were you running, that you'd need someone like Moose for?"

"Nothing illegal, I can assure you, but sometimes it helps to have a big guy around. I had to deal with some union guys. But no, our business was office products. Plastic desk accessories. You know, those stackable letter trays, the little gizmos that hold paper clips, pen-and-pencil cups. That kind of thing."

I glanced down at my desk. There was a phone, a laptop, a yellow legal pad, a few pens scattered haphazardly nearby, and a *grande* cup of Starbucks that had grown lukewarm. No desk accessories. I probably had some paper clips somewhere, but they were most likely in my top drawer. I didn't bother to look.

"Okay."

"My ex's family started the business. Suzy's grandfather actually. He was an engineer, he began by making plastic containers for cosmetics companies. After a while, the cosmetics companies found it cheaper to buy their containers overseas. The Orientals can do everything cheaper."

"I believe they prefer to be called Asians now," I gently pointed out.

Phil Zellis shrugged. "Who cares what they want. They were going to put Suzy's family out of business. My father-in-law noticed that most of the desk accessories back in the day were made out of metal. He figured, why not come out with a line made of plastic. More colorful, nicer design. They already had the injection-molding machines, they could make plastic look like anything. Worked out. The business took off."

"And then he brought you in."

"Yeah, after Suzy and I graduated, I needed a job, and I needed to support a family. She didn't have a head for business, she majored in art history, can you believe that? Her father took me in and taught me the ropes. Then he had a heart attack at age forty-five. Her grandfather had retired by then, and I think he was also developing Alzheimer's. She didn't have any brothers or sisters, and her cousins were a bunch of entitled idiots who didn't want to work for a living. So it fell on me. All of a sudden, at age twenty-five, I'm running a multimillion-dollar business."

"You fell into something good."

"Yeah. Went well for quite a while. But you know, nothing lasts forever in this world."

I decided not to probe any further on Phil's family business for now. I also decided to look further into Moose.

"Okay," I said. "If your daughter filed a police report, there's something to work with. But I'll need a few things."

"Like what?"

"Mostly contact info for your daughter, the boyfriend, your ex-wife. You have a current wife?"

Phil looked at me. "Yeah. But I don't call her that."

"I wouldn't either. Plus, how to contact Moose. And maybe your father, too, you can never tell what other family members know. Your dad still live in Culver City?" I asked.

"Yeah, but not in the same place. He's retired. Lives up on Culver Crest now."

I nodded. Culver Crest was the ritzy part of Culver City, up on a hill, with a view. It was nothing compared to Beverly Hills or a lot of other tony Westside neighborhoods, but as far as Culver City went, this was pricey real estate.

"Your dad must have done well. For a public servant."

"You'd be surprised at how well cops do in retirement these days. He got a big payout when he retired from Largo Beach. Something to do with disability. Nice pension takes care of expenses. And his trips to Vegas."

I thought about this. When we were growing up, there was always something unseemly about Phil's father. Police officers were paid well compared to other civil servants, but they were hardly at the level of investment bankers. Yet Phil's father always seemed to be driving a new car, while my mom struggled to make payments on a fifteen-year-old Honda Civic. And Phil's family often went to Cabo or Maui for vacations; we drove down to San Diego if we went anywhere at all. And there was the issue of attending Vassar College, where tuition was close to what my mother made in a year. Things didn't add up.

"All right. I'll poke around and see what I find. You know about my fee?"

Phil smiled slyly. "You mean, you're not going to do a solid for an old high school teammate?"

"No."

The smile disappeared. "How much?"

"A thousand dollars a day. And I require a two-day retainer. We'll see what I come up with. You'll get your money's worth. Most people do."

He reluctantly reached into his pocket, pulled out a checkbook, and began scribbling. "You know, ever since we sold the business a few years ago, I've been a little more aware of money. Got a big pile of it, but no more coming in. It's all just going out."

I decided not to sympathize. Phil Zellis could surely make do with his big pile.

"Here you go," he said, then stood up to leave. "I assume I'll be hearing from you in a couple of days."

"You will."

"Look, I know it's been years since we've gotten together, but I've always thought of you as a friend. I hope now that I'm employing you and paying you good money, well, I hope it doesn't affect our friendship."

"Why do you bring that up?" I frowned.

"I've had a few friendships that went south after we established a business relationship. The people thought my paying them somehow diminished them in my eyes. I hope you don't feel that way."

"Not at all," I said, as I peeked at the check before folding it in half and putting it in my pocket. "In fact, I think our relationship just got a whole lot better."

Two

After doing an exhaustive search, I found out nothing more about the Amanda Zeal incident. I spoke with Drew Slick, a detective I knew at the Beverly Hills Police Department, and managed to uncover little of substance. After a good bit of reminiscing and false flattery, Detective Slick told me that yes, an assault had taken place, a report had been filed, a unit had been deployed to the scene, and an investigation was ongoing. But no, I couldn't have any more details. And yes, Slick said, it sure was a pleasure to hear from me.

I grabbed a quick lunch at a high-end taco truck parked outside of my office building. It was high-end because they had a phone app and a lengthy menu featuring a remarkable variety of tacos, ones stuffed with everything from calamari to short ribs. Avocado, pepper jack cheese and Korean kimchi were available as extra toppings for a not-so-small fee. The days of food trucks being referred to as roach coaches were over; the new world order had indeed begun. I asked for a pair of tacos with *carnitas*, unencumbered by pricey add-ons, and ate them while sitting on the curb. They weren't fantastic, they weren't bad. They were simply what passed for lunch these days.

Moose Machado lived in a ramshackle apartment building along Pico, just east of Alvarado in downtown L.A., not far from Staples Center. It was a tan brick building, the type of shabby building developers stopped putting up after the 1930s, as brick structures would often crumble during an earthquake. The ones that were already built simply remained, occupied by the people who could not afford to live anywhere else.

Moose's building was called a mixed-use dwelling, a form of development that was having a renaissance in L.A. these days. The apartments were located above a group of family-run businesses, ones that included a liquor store, a barber shop, and the office of an immigration attorney. The liquor store had one of those Plexiglas partitions that separates the customers from the cashiers to minimize the opportunity for successful armed robberies. But despite the mixed-use format becoming more in vogue now, this particular neighborhood remained all too slum-like. The sidewalks were scattered with litter, there was brightly colored graffiti along the sides of the building, and each storefront had a metal guard door that was pulled down each night. The metal protector was rarely seen in nicer neighborhoods, those where broken windows and ransacked shops were not a regular part of life. This was the type of neighborhood you were either born in, or otherwise tumbled down into when your money ran out.

I walked up a rickety staircase and noticed the pungent smell of what were probably tamales, and not very good tamales. I rapped on apartment number four and the door opened a few seconds later. Standing before me was the equivalent of a human dump truck, a massive slab of a human being that seemed almost as wide as he was tall. He had a thick pile of unkempt black hair, a pockmarked complexion, and he wore a decades-old t-shirt that promoted Al Gore for President.

"Moose Machado?" I asked.

"Who wants to know?" he shot back.

"Name's Burnside. We knew each other a long time ago. High school."

The Moose peered out for a long moment, striving to see if he recognized me. It didn't look good. Then a warm smile crossed his face, and it was as if twenty-five years just melted away.

"Burnside. Crap. I remember. The football team at Culver."

"Right," I said. "Mind if I come in?"

He opened the door wider and I slipped past his massive girth. The apartment was small, and it was over-furnished with a hodgepodge of aging furniture, faded, yellowing pictures of family, and a variety of Jesus knick-knacks – Jesus strapped to a wooden cross, Jesus standing in a large glass-enclosed candle, Jesus hovering on a wall painting and Jesus looking out from a large piece of stained glass hung over a window. Moose picked up a newspaper from a deceptively soft orange couch and pointed for me to sit. I sat.

"How you been, man?" he asked. "Dang, if it hasn't been a

David Chill

long time."

"I'm good. Looks like you left Culver City."

"Yeah, I've bounced around," Moose said. "You want a beer or something?"

"No, thanks," I said, looking down at my watch. It was one-thirty in the afternoon. "How long you been down here?"

"Maybe a couple years. This used to be my grandma's apartment before she passed. It's on rent control, so I'm not paying much. I got some money problems."

"Sorry to hear."

"Yeah, sounds like you've done okay. Cop, detective, football coach. Was freaky when I was watching a USC game on TV a few years ago and saw you on the sideline. I only know a couple famous people."

"I'm a very minor celebrity," I chuckled, thinking maybe Moose hadn't read the newspaper accounts of my getting kicked off the LAPD a decade ago. Being famous for the wrong reasons had more than its share of drawbacks.

"So, what brings you down here, man?" he asked.

"Phil Zellis."

"Oh yeah. I heard from Phil this morning. He said he was hiring a guy to look into what happened with Amanda. I guess that's you."

"Guess so."

"Yeah. I'm going over to Amanda's apartment tonight to look out for her."

"You work for Phil a lot?"

"Here and there."

I looked at Moose and then gave his small living quarters the once-over. I wondered what twist of fate deposited

Moose in these threadbare surroundings, and got a strong feeling they were of his own making. When people hit bottom, there's normally a good reason for their fall, and it's usually their own doing.

"Okay. Got any ideas about what's happening with his daughter?" I asked.

Moose said nothing for a long moment. I briefly wondered if I should rephrase the question to one that might be easier to grasp, but he finally licked his lips and began to speak.

"I know Phil doesn't trust this new boyfriend of hers. Wyatt I think his name is. But Phil doesn't know the half of Amanda. He and his wife weren't around much when she was growing up. I don't even know why those two stayed married as long as they did. Phil had me look after Amanda a bunch of times when she was in high school, Phil was like, too busy. I got to know her a little. Nice kid, but wild. Lots of money. Throw in some bad friends, and you got a problem."

I frowned. "Bad friends, huh? Is Beverly Hills High a rough school these days?"

Moose laughed. "Phil's kids didn't go there. I guess if you can afford a big house in Beverly Hills, you can afford private school. Amanda and her little brother went to some ritzy school in Santa Monica. Lot of snotty friends. If you can call them friends."

"How so?"

"I don't know. She's a good looking girl you know, but I guess she liked to get guys hot and then not pay off. Do it enough times and something happens. I've seen it before. Used to work security at the Peppermint Rhino."

I stifled a frown. The Peppermint Rhino was a chain of

strip clubs on the west coast. I motioned for Moose to continue; I didn't need him to go into the details of his other line of work. I had been to a few of these clubs, mostly tagging along on bachelor parties. Without the benefits of alcohol-infused haziness, I found most of them to be a little depressing.

"Yeah, well, in Amanda's case, she was on the school swim team, she told me she was a really good swimmer, said she had a shot at the Olympics or something before she hurt her arm. Don't know if that was true or not. Anyways, someone snuck in the locker room and shot a video of her getting undressed. Who knows, maybe it was another girl who did it, but the video ended up on the internet. Got everyone upset, the school, the parents, it was a big deal there. Someone got it pulled down pretty quick. No one got caught. Funny thing though, the only person who wasn't upset about it was Amanda."

"She wanted the attention?" I asked, rather sure I knew the answer. If Amanda was like a lot of girls who grew up with too much money and not enough parenting. She probably had some yearning that went unfulfilled, and perhaps relished being the girl everyone talked about. It didn't really matter what was being said. For some people, any publicity was good publicity.

"I guess. She got offers to be on a bunch of college swim teams, ended up at Stanford. Didn't quite swim as well as when she was sixteen, maybe she never got over that injury. But that didn't stop her from strutting her stuff. This time the videos that went up on the internet was mostly her looking hot in a bathing suit. She got some modeling gigs, I don't know if she even graduated, but Fox hired her to be on TV for football games. You know. Interview the coaches at halftime, the star players at the end of the game. She says there have been a few issues, though. I guess that's why Phil brought me in again."

"How's that?"

"Amanda's getting a lot of attention. With that comes the usual nut jobs. She's had a few stalkers over the years. I've had to step in and deal with them. Among my other jobs for Phil."

"What did you do for Amanda before? Push a few of those tough prep school kids around?"

Moose gave a small smile. "That was the fun part. Kids who're born rich aren't always born smart. Or maybe they thought they could act tough because their dad's got money. They thought wrong. They got the type of lesson kids normally learn on the streets."

"Guys have been bothering Amanda since she was a teenager, then."

"Yeah. Like I says, she's had a few stalkers. I slapped them around a little. Didn't take much to get the message through. And I got the feeling no one ever taught 'em any manners. I taught 'em a few. And they stayed away from Amanda after that. Far away."

"You ever talk to Amanda about her own behavior? That maybe she was bringing this on?"

Moose looked away. "No. And I don't think it would have mattered much. Some girls just get off this way."

"You think the guy that attacked her was a stalker?" I asked.

He thought about this for a few seconds. "Don't know, man. But there were two of them this time. Makes me think not. Stalkers, nah. They just want the girl for themselves. They're usually loners."

I was impressed with his answer. "Sounds like you have some good detective chops. You ever work in law enforcement?"

Moose nodded. "For about a year. Was with the County Sheriff's department. Good job, but pretty demanding."

"Most jobs are demanding. What happened?"

"Got into it with my sergeant. I'm not real good at taking orders."

"Me neither," I said, starting to wonder how much more I had in common with Moose, and shuddering again at his surroundings. This was the kind of dump I used to wonder if I'd end up in. That was years ago though, before I met Gail, before we had Marcus, and before I started to make some good money. But the fears you once had never fully leave you; they just get pushed into the recesses of your mind, quietly lurking, albeit distant.

"Okay," I said and handed Moose my card. "Give me a call if anything happens. Or if you need some backup."

"Sure," Moose said, fingering the card carefully. "Hey, before you go, I'm wondering if you might be able to help me out of a jam. You being former LAPD and all."

"What's that?" I asked tentatively.

"I owe some money to a guy. He's connected. I'm having trouble paying him back, and he's making demands."

"How did you come to owe him money?"

"Lost a few bets. I was having a really good run on football this year. But the last month of the season, everything went bad."

"How much are we talking here?"

"Twenty large."

I sat back. "Twenty thousand is a lot of money. How'd you get that far into debt?"

Moose clenched his right fist and then opened it again. "Made some bad wagers, so I began betting more to make up for them. Didn't work. That just dropped me deeper in the hole."

"You ask Phil for help?"

"Yeah, but he's not being real generous. Believes people have to solve their own problems."

"What do you want from me?" I asked.

"Maybe get them to back off for a little while until I can pay them their vig. I'll get 'em their money, but you know, it's just going to take some time. People like this aren't real good at listening to sob stories. They want their money right away, or else. Doesn't matter how big you are, they can cut anyone down to size."

"What's their name?"

"Name's Mike White. Has a bunch of goons doing the collections for him. They're not good at listening to reason, either."

I glanced out the window. Across the street, a taco truck was parked in front of a nail salon. It didn't look high-end. I doubted they had calamari tacos on the menu.

"I can maybe try and talk to them. But don't expect much. If they're not worried about a guy like you, they're probably not going to worry about a guy like me."

"Yeah," Moose said as he handed me a white slip of paper with a phone number scrawled on it. "But you're all I got right now."

*

The drive back to the Westside was a breeze, as it often is for about a one-hour window each day. The trick is being lucky enough to zoom onto the 10 freeway during that particular narrow stretch of time, which has an unnerving habit of changing daily. Today, that hour was 2:00 pm. The skies were clear, a soft breeze was blowing, and the temperature was in the high 60s . If you had to endure a January day and could time the freeway traffic just right, there were few places better to live in than southern California.

I exited at Overland, and drove south for a couple of miles through Culver City. Like Beverly Hills and Santa Monica, Culver City butted up against the city of Los Angeles, giving it civic boundaries that were confusing to everyone including police officers. It had its own municipal government, police force, and civic pride, although much of that pride emanated from the famed MGM studios. I knew something about Culver City, for I had spent the first eighteen years of my life here.

Unlike Santa Monica, which could be characterized as an upscale coastal city, or Beverly Hills, which housed some of the wealthiest people on earth, Culver City was a maze of contradictions. It was the glitzy home to the Sony studios, purchased from MGM decades earlier, but it was also a bedroom community, with modest single-family houses and utilitarian apartment buildings. Culver City had developed a burgeoning downtown, replete with trendy restaurants, brew pubs, multiplex theaters, and art galleries. But the south end of town was home to various downscale strip malls that featured check cashing stores, massage parlors, and the types of bars where not many patrons could accurately define what a craft beer was. It was a city that was trying to shed its working-class roots and doing an uneven job of it.

I didn't really know who to talk to next, so I stopped off at a Starbucks in downtown Culver City to mull things over. Every table was filled. I took my *grande* Italian roast and strode down the street, winding up in the lobby of the Culver Hotel. A nicely dressed bellhop in a gray outfit asked if I was checking in, and I told him I was just waiting for someone. He said all right and walked away. I strolled to an overstuffed couch and sat down. The couch was big and comfy, with a number of soft pillows tossed about, and it faced a series of large bay windows where a rush of sunlight poured in. The ceiling was twenty-five-feet high, and a half-dozen elegant chandeliers hung from it.

The Culver Hotel has been around for nearly a century and was built by the same Harry Culver after whom the city was named. The hotel was a big deal back then, when the nearby MGM studios hit their heyday. The place wound up having many owners, and legend had it that a previous proprietor, Charlie Chaplin, once lost the establishment to John Wayne in a poker match. The Duke was so impressed with his newfound status as a hotel squire that he immediately donated the building to a charity. Over the years the hotel, not surprisingly with its varied and uninvolved ownership, had fallen into disrepair; some people even whispered it was haunted. But a few years ago, new buyers purchased the place, fixed things up, and it suddenly experienced a renaissance as a trendy boutique hotel.

Sipping my coffee, I worked my iPad. Through LinkedIn, I learned Wyatt Angstrom was a senior vice president with Fox Television. The specifics of his position were vague, something about aligning digital strategies and new technologies into a revenue-based marketing platform. I took that to mean he had a rather boring career, because my mind began to wander halfway through reading his job description. He had graduated fifteen years ago from a university in Florida that I had never heard of.

I called the Fox general number, and was rerouted a half-dozen times. I finally got through to Wyatt Angstrom, who, after placing me on hold for five minutes, came back on and said he would be able to see me first thing in the morning. I asked what first thing in the morning meant in his world and he told me nine-thirty. I called the Fox number again and asked for Grady Pinn, the college football broadcaster, but the transfer put me straight to voice mail. I left a message and wondered if he would ever get it.

I continued to cruise the internet, finding out little more about Wyatt Angstrom, but there was a treasure trove of slinky photos and salacious gossip about Amanda Zeal. The photos were the standard swimsuit shots, but the scuttlebutt ranged from romantic involvement to testy altercations with a number of current pro football players. The one name that jumped out at me was Xavier Bishop, a former USC football player I had met a few years ago. X was now playing for the Buffalo Bills, which meant his season was now over, as the playoffs had begun. I did a search on him and saw that he lived in nearby Baldwin Hills, noting the address. I called the phone number I had, and left a message.

It was now almost four, and I had run out of things to do today for Phil Zellis. I drove home to an empty house, empty only because Gail was still at work and Marcus had a play date at the Hartnetts, our new neighbors who had a son Marcus's age. I strolled into their backyard and watched Marcus kick a soccer ball back and forth with his new friend, Brendan. After a couple of minutes, he managed to notice me.

"Daddy!"

"Good kicking, Marcus," I said, giving him a hug when he ran up to me.

"I think we got a pair of future strikers here," said Will Hartnett, walking over and shaking my hand.

It goes without saying that my preference for Marcus's athletic future would have been to strike down opposing ball carriers, or to dart downfield, plucking a tight spiral out of the air. It seemed, though, he'd rather simply kick a defenseless soccer ball. I regularly got him to play catch with me in our backyard, throwing a football back and forth, but I think I got more fun out of it than he did. Kids often decide what sport is right for them. In our case, however, the decider might be my wife, Gail, who exhibited little interest in seeing Marcus don a helmet and delve into battle.

"I'm glad they're enjoying themselves," I managed. "Thanks for taking him after school."

"Not a problem," he said. "I work from home, so this is a nice break."

"What do you do?"

"I'm a day trader."

"Ah," I said, thinking that job was not far removed from being a professional gambler. "How's the market?"

"Down for most of the day. Recovered in the last hour, so I made some money. Good day overall."

"Beats a bad day."

"Yeah," he said. "Hey, I read a few minutes ago that there's going to be an opening in the City Attorney's office."

"Oh?" I said. Will Hartnett was well aware Gail worked as an Assistant City Attorney. "Someone get caught with their hand in the cookie jar?"

"Nah. Mayor's office is open. The City Attorney, Jay Sutker. He's announced he's going to run. I don't know if he'll win, but it means the City Attorney job is going to be vacant. Gail going to throw her hat in the ring?"

I gave the standard palms-up sign to signify I had no idea, which was about as honest a reaction as I could muster. Gail and I had never talked directly about this, but I knew she had an interest in politics, and I knew she would be terrific at most anything she set her mind to do. I also knew I would be an albatross around her beautiful neck.

"She's good, my friend. Let me know if she's running. I'm happy to volunteer."

"I'll remember that," I said, and signaled to Marcus that it was time to go home.

"Aw, do I have to?" he said, glumly.

"Well, I thought maybe you could help me surprise Mom

with dinner."

"Oh, yeah? What are we having?"

"Maybe we can barbecue some hamburgers."

"Yay! I love those!"

Will Hartnett laughed at Marcus's exuberance. "Enjoy them. Nothing beats L.A. in January. Back home in Chicago, we don't break out the barbecues until May. Otherwise, we'd be brushing snow off the lids."

"I can only imagine," I said. Marcus and I headed across the street into our house and then out onto the back patio. I pulled the cover off of our grill and piled some charcoal briquettes into a metal cylinder, stuffing a few pieces of newspaper in the bottom and lighting it with a match. Gail always chided me for not buying a gas barbecue, pointing out that charcoal took too long to get hot, and created too much smoke. I would listen politely and smile to myself. The complaining always stopped when she bit into dinner. There are benefits to being old-school.

After I insisted that he wash his hands thoroughly with soap, Marcus helped out with dinner by throwing a carefully measured handful of seasoning into the pile of ground beef, mixing it up, and then trying to mold the meat into patties. The shapes invariably looked nothing like a hamburger. After he was finished with his handiwork, which better resembled a few bizarre dinosaurs than anything close to conventional food, I took over and smacked the concoction back and forth in my palms, bringing them into burger-like form.

We were getting ready to place the meat on the grill when Gail arrived. She swept Marcus up into her arms and gave him a kiss before setting him back down. She then wrapped her arms around my neck and kissed me.

"I'm second now, huh?" I said with a hint of petulance.

"You're both first," she smiled. "Marcus is just easier to lift."

"He is."

"And I love that my boys are making dinner."

"You know the secret to making good barbecued burgers?"

"Do tell."

"You never push the hamburgers down with a spatula. I've seen lots of people do this. The grease squirts into the coals and it sparks a fire which chars the meat. But all the juice leaks out that way and you end up with a dry burger."

"Funny how you never mentioned that before."

"I have to hold some things confidential. Keeps the spark in a marriage. That way, you're always learning new things."

"I certainly am," she smiled. "And what else are we having besides burgers?"

I looked down at Marcus and he looked up at me. Neither of us said a word, although the expressions on our faces probably spoke volumes. We looked over at Gail simultaneously. "I guess we hadn't gotten that far planning the menu."

"Let me see what I can scrounge up," she said and walked into the house.

By the time the burgers were done, Gail had already made a salad and microwaved some tater tots. The burgers came out juicy, and as we dug in, we asked Marcus about his day, mostly learning all about his soccer practice and a girl in his preschool class who kept bothering him. I told Marcus it was because the girl liked him and wanted his attention, and I smiled at his vehement denials. After we finished, Marcus went off to watch TV, and Gail and I began to do the dishes.

"I understand there was some news today."

Gail turned to me. "You heard about Sutker."

"I did. Have you known about this?"

"I heard the rumors a few days ago. But he's mostly kept it under wraps."

"What do you think?"

"I think he's got a chance to be mayor."

I rubbed my eyes. "Who do you think will replace him in your office?"

Gail dried her hands and turned toward me. "I sense what you're thinking."

"Okay. Please tell me, because I'm honestly not so certain myself."

Gail watched me for a long moment. Her clear gray eyes, the eyes that always reminded me of soft, spring raindrops, no longer looked very clear and no longer looked very soft. Her eyes, of course, didn't really change, but rather the expression around them, the unspoken communication that sometimes reveals a person's soul. There was a stirring inside of Gail, something different, an anxiety perhaps, a sense that her world was not as assured as it had been.

"This is an opportunity that may not come again for another eight years," she started. "Maybe longer."

"I know. Running for City Attorney is a big deal."

"If I run and win, our lives will change."

"Yes," I agreed.

Her lips closed tightly for a second. "I can't do it if you're not for it. And if you're okay with the scrutiny this will bring on us."

It was my turn to take a long pause. "I don't want to hold you back. But I don't want you to get tarred with the same brush that took down my career as a police officer. That will come up in the campaign. It's almost guaranteed. Politics is a dirty business. Especially in L.A."

"I have no problems with your past. You know what really happened and so do I. You did nothing wrong."

"But you're aware of the business I'm in. I sometimes have to investigate some nasty people. And it can occasionally get in the papers. It hasn't been a big deal before this. A few people you work with probably know, but most don't. That will change."

"I'm aware of that."

"And I think that's why you never took the name Burnside. You still go by Gail Pepper."

"I didn't do it because of what I was afraid people might think," she said. "I did it because it's how I became known in law school and as a young attorney. I didn't think it was important to take your name. But we never discussed it. I never brought it up and neither did you. So let me ask you now. Do *you* think it's important?"

I shook my head. "Of all the things in the world to worry about, that's way down on the list. Probably at the bottom."

"Good," she sighed.

"And just so you know, the name Pepper describes you well. Pretty hot."

Gail smiled for what seemed like the first time in an eternity, although it probably was just a few minutes. "You know, there will be a lot of attorneys dipping their toes in the water here. Seeing if they want to jump into the race. And there are certainly no guarantees I'll win. I very well might lose."

"Life is full of uncertainty. But better to know than to not know. Maybe that's why Sutker is running for mayor. You only get a few shots at the brass ring. If you decide to wait, the opportunity might not be there later. If it's your time, you want to seize the moment. You don't want it to pass."

"True," she said.

"Sutker may have some trouble getting elected mayor, as well. I've heard Arthur Woo is planning to run."

"How do you know this? Local politics isn't really your thing."

"You recall I met with Arthur recently. I had a few questions regarding that case I worked on, the one featuring our dearly departed city councilman. The late Colin Glasscock. Arthur casually mentioned the mayor was termed out this year. Arthur's ambitious. He said you were, too."

"Oh?" Gail said, eyebrows raised. "I didn't think he'd remember me. We've only met a few times. The first time was at that debate where his brother was up against Rex Palmer."

"You made a lasting impression apparently," I said, thinking it was interesting how some women had an ungodly lack of awareness of the impact they had on men. Gail was one of them. Beautiful on the outside, but not really cognizant of her beauty. She just didn't seem to think about it much.

"I guess I have some goals for myself. But it's not really about career advancement or acquiring power. The City

Attorney's office could be run a lot better. Less infighting. More technological progress. And I'm not sure the other candidates who'll run for the job have an interest in doing that. To some people, it's a stepping stone to the next level."

"Like being mayor," I observed.

Gail tried to push back the smile. "Perhaps. My boss has made no bones about the fact that he'd like to be running things at City Hall. For him, the mayor's job has always been in his sights. And maybe statewide office after that. He's not a bad guy, but there have been some ugly rumors about him. And he often makes decisions that are aimed at improving his public profile, not what's best for prosecuting criminals."

"Mommy," came a voice from behind us. We turned and looked at Marcus.

"Sweetie, how long have you been listening to us?" Gail asked.

"I dunno," he said. "But what's a mayor do?"

"A mayor," Gail answered, "is like the leader of the city. He makes important decisions."

"Does he own the city?"

"No," she said. "He just tries to help people. My boss is going to try and be mayor. Don't you think that's exciting?"

"Brendan's dad says the mayor's a crook. Is your boss a crook, too?"

Gail looked at me and I shrugged in response. I decided to let the silver-tongued politician respond to that one, and she took Marcus aside for a chat. My suspicion was that might take a little while. I opened the refrigerator, took out a bottle of Blue Moon, and walked into the den. Marcus had been watching a cartoon featuring two characters battling each other with light sabers. I changed it to a sports channel that featured a group of former football players arguing and yelling about who would be playing in the Super Bowl in a few weeks. The difference between the two shows seemed minimal at best. I sat back to watch, but found myself listening more to Gail and Marcus.

"I wouldn't call him a crook, Marcus," Gail said slowly, her tone being careful and measured. "Not exactly."

Three

Mid-January in Los Angeles can bring forth a wide range of weather, but it is rarely bad weather. We've had occasional hot days that get up into the 90s, and torrential rainstorms where the water practically comes down in sheets. We can even get temperatures that dip into the frigid range, although for Los Angeles, frigid is mostly defined as slipping below 50 degrees. We rarely get snow and we never get blizzards. What we normally get in January are days like today. Cool mornings that start in the mid-50s, evolving into mild afternoons that settle pleasantly into the high-60s. Gail calls it sweater weather. I would too, except I don't wear sweaters. A jacket does a far superior job of camouflaging the .357 tucked surreptitiously into the nylon mesh holster underneath my armpit.

I arrived at the Fox lot on Pico at ten after nine. My name was on the invited list of guests, which meant the security guard was friendly when he directed me toward the garage. There had been instances when I entered a studio lot and was not treated so friendly. Even with an LAPD badge, security was reluctant to allow me in without my name appearing on the special list. A brief discussion about the jail time waiting for those interfering with law enforcement duties often finished that conversation.

Another security guard waved for me to stop as I pulled up to the garage. He instructed me to pop the trunk of my Pathfinder, but knowing the handle was notoriously difficult to locate, I got out and walked around to show him personally. Lifting the back door up, I pointed to the empty gasoline can, jumper cables, a half-full gallon of windshield washer fluid, and the earthquake bag Gail packed and then repacked each year for me. It was an unremarkable pile of gear that would likely injure no one, except possibly myself.

"Everything look okay?" I asked.

The guard reached over and unzipped the earthquake bag and briefly rummaged through it. Finding little more than a blanket, bottled water and some canned food, he re-zipped it and nodded approvingly at me.

"You're good," he said.

"Still getting terrorist threats these days?"

"We get threats, but they're almost always just that. I doubt they're from terrorists, though."

"Who are they from?"

"Probably screenwriters," he smiled, giving me a wink. "And the occasional studio exec that's been fired. Lots of guys that talk tough. But that's all it normally is. Talk."

I nodded in return, hopped into my vehicle and drove inside. The garage was big and roomy, and the spaces were wider than most parking structures offered. There was a distinctive odor, not of gasoline fumes, but more like fresh paint. Most of the cars were late model, with an abundance of Mercedes, Lexuses, and BMWs. This seemed like a nice place to park, although finding an open space proved a challenge, with the visitors' spaces all filled up. An executive once told me that employees often grabbed these spots, as they were closer to the elevators, saving time when people were running late. It was another reminder that people who worked in show business were just a little different.

My phone buzzed, and when I picked up, I was treated to the silky smooth voice of Grady Pinn. There are some sportscasters who were born to have a microphone in their hands, and Grady was one of them. I told him I had just arrived on the studio lot, and asked if we could get together and talk this morning. He told me to meet him at the commissary at eleven.

Wyatt Angstrom's office was on the sixth floor of a new office tower. The tower had an exterior of blue glass and a large lobby that featured a wall full of TVs, all tuned to different cable channels. I rode up a smartly designed elevator with a dozen other people, none of whom spoke to one another, all silently glancing down at their phones, some moving their thumbs rapidly. I found Wyatt's office after a few minutes of walking aimlessly around the sixth floor, finally breaking down and asking someone for directions. Wyatt's assistant's desk was situated directly outside his door. The assistant's nameplate said his name was Dirk, and he looked like he was barely out of college. He was listening to someone talk in rapid-fire staccato on his phone, glancing up at me briefly as he took notes. I waited a good five minutes until the call was completed. Even then, it took another ten seconds for him to acknowledge me, just as I was starting to feel my level of irritation rising.

"May I help you?"

"I'm Burnside. I have an appointment with Wyatt."

"Oh," he said, looking into his computer screen. "Funny, I don't have you down on Mr. Angstrom's calendar."

"Yeah, that's funny."

"No, I really don't see you on there."

"And I really don't care. Can you please tell Wyatt I'm here?"

"I need to figure this out."

"No you don't," I said. "Just go ask him."

"What is this regarding?" he inquired.

"It's a personal matter. He may want to keep it private."

"Oh. And just what is the reason for your visit?"

I gave him a long look. That intimidated some people, but Dirk wasn't one of them. Maybe he was used to people posturing. Maybe he was just numb.

"Like I said. My visit is personal. It's not something Mr. Angstrom would want me to discuss," I said, wondering at what point I would grab him by the front of his shirt and shove him up against a wall. My sense was that it might be coming soon.

"Well, I'm Mr. Angstrom's personal assistant, so I ... "

"Dirk!"

We both turned to look at a short, muscular man, about forty years old, with an intense look on his face. He had a bandage above his chin and one of his eyes appeared red and swollen. He didn't look happy.

"I'll see this Mr. Burnside. And Dirk, next time someone tells you they have a personal matter to discuss with me, you can assume it's a subject that they don't need to discuss with you."

"Yes, Mr. Angstrom, I only ... "

"Mr. Burnside, please come inside," Wyatt Angstrom said brusquely, in a voice that was louder than necessary, one that served the dual purpose of shutting down his assistant and letting him know who was the boss. He shot Dirk a final glance before turning and following me.

His office was large and plush. The desk was big and was probably made from oak. Numerous plaques hung on the wall, and there were some framed posters as well. The windows faced east with a distant view of downtown, and striped sunlight peeked in through the mini-blinds. The carpet was thick and surprisingly deep. Wyatt Angstrom walked behind his desk, and motioned for me to sit in one of the black chairs facing him. The chair looked beautiful but it was hard as a rock. I shifted to get comfortable.

"Sorry about my assistant," he said. "Everyone wants to get a job at a studio, but they don't know how to act once they get here. You're lucky if you can find one who isn't a jerk."

I looked at him and responded with a tired bromide. "I'm sure good help is hard to find."

"Yes," he said and got right down to business. "I understand Amanda's father hired you. He called me last night. Said that you're a detective of some sort, and you two were friends. Go way back."

"High school football," I said, not bothering to correct him about being friends. "I'm a licensed private investigator."

"Impressive," he responded, his tone sounding dry. "I'd like to find out what happened the other night, too."

"Tell me about it," I said in a short, clipped manner. If Wyatt Angstrom was going to dispense with pleasantries, I would, too.

Angstrom shook his head. "Not totally sure, exactly. Couple of gangsters followed us back to Amanda's place after dinner. They jumped us."

"Gangsters?"

"They were Hispanic," he said, running his fingers through some thinning hair. "They looked the part."

I didn't bother to let him continue down the path of typecasting people. "They get any valuables?" I asked.

Wyatt Angstrom rubbed the left side of his face. It was a rugged face, both handsome and ugly at the same time. He had thinning hair and small eyes. He wore a tailored, button-down white shirt with the letters WHA monogrammed just above the cuff, and he had on a nondescript blue tie.

"Nothing was stolen, and that's the weird thing. It never got that far. In fact, everything happened really fast. We were just walking along one minute, and the next this white van pulls up beside us and these two *cholos* jump out. They didn't demand anything, they just attacked us. One of them grabbed my arms, the other started to pummel me. If I had been ready, I would have kicked their butts. They weren't that big. But they got the jump on me, and I got knocked down to the pavement. Then they went after Amanda."

"What do you mean 'went after her'?" I frowned.

"Grabbed her. Punched her in the face. Looked like they

might have been trying to drag her into the van. By the time I got to her, she already had her pepper spray out. Sprayed one of them full in the face. Scared the other one enough for him to back off and head for the van."

"That's what it took for them to go? Nailing them with some pepper spray?"

"You ever get hit with that stuff? It's nasty. I punched the other guy a couple of times, but he kicked me in the groin and got away."

"Oh," I managed. "So what did they look like?"

"Like I said, Hispanics of some sort. I don't know, Mexican, whatever, we got 'em all here. I didn't get to see their visas. Probably illegals. You know. L.A. and all."

"Uh-huh," I said. "And what happened next?"

"The other guy managed to stumble back into the van. They took off, although the van was weaving all over the road. I don't know how they managed to drive like that. I made the mistake of putting my hands on my face afterward, and some of that pepper spray wound up on me. It took like an hour of flushing my eye with water before the stinging eased up."

"Can you describe the van?"

"Just a white van, it might have had the name of a rental agency on it. Maybe Star Rentals. Didn't even see what model it was. The street was kind of dark, too."

"So, no robbery attempt," I mused.

"Nope. Didn't seem like they were after money."

"What do you think they were after?"

"Amanda."

I raised my eyebrows. "Really?"

"Yeah. Her dad's rich and she's pretty. And famous. I would think her dad would pay a lot of money to get her back. The network might, too. She's a hot commodity."

I started wondering how the conversation had veered off into this direction. Kidnapping an adult is usually rare and usually fails. It requires a detailed plan, complete with how to pick up the money and return the victim without getting caught. Since kidnappings typically involve large ransoms, the FBI often gets involved. And unless the victim is blindfolded, releasing them allows for an eyewitness to provide a detailed description of the culprits. As a result, the majority of kidnapping victims are simply never heard from again, regardless of whether or not the ransom is paid. I always thought there were far easier ways to steal money without the risk of having it escalate into homicide.

"Just how confident are you that this was a kidnapping attempt?"

Angstrom smirked. "How confident can you really be? I mean, I was confident my second wife wouldn't leave me. But I still made her sign a pre-nup."

I took this in and felt like shaking my head. I resisted the urge. "You been seeing Amanda for a while?"

"Almost six months."

"You two serious?"

Wyatt Angstrom gave the hint of a smirk, but then caught himself. "Sure. About as serious as anyone is in L.A. when it comes to dating."

"Who'd she go out with before you?"

Any further hint of a smirk disappeared at that moment, it was as if some alternative being had reached over and wiped his face clean of the arrogance. He wasn't expecting the question. His mouth opened and he paused a long moment, so I looked around his spacious office. It was a nice office, with framed posters of old TV shows. One was from the old series, Dragnet, and featured a close-up of a stone-faced Jack Webb. He didn't look happy, either.

"Amanda," he began, "has had an on-again, off-again relationship with this guy. Mostly it's been off. But she's been screwing him since she was sixteen."

"She told you this?"

"It came out eventually, mostly in dribs and drabs. She didn't want to tell me. I don't blame her. And that's why I'm a little concerned."

"You think this ex-boyfriend is behind it?"

"I don't know. But he calls her sometimes. She's got this love-hate thing going with him. It extends to her family somehow, she's been reluctant to get into too many details. The guy isn't real trustworthy, at least he didn't strike me as such when I met him."

"When did you meet him?" I asked.

"Some family event her father had. Maybe a month ago. The guy's a bruiser, and he was giving me the evil eye all night. Like I had intruded on his territory or something. But I mean, man, it's just women. There's a million hot girls in L.A. I don't know what his problem was."

"So you talked to Amanda about him."

"Afterwards, yeah. I figured any boyfriend she was banging at one time wouldn't be around anymore. And I think she still had feelings for him, although she denies it. He didn't strike me as her type of guy. I mean, crap, he's twice her age. But some girls like that. And I guess this Anthony Machado still likes her. He's got a weird nickname. Moose."

*

I left the blue glass tower scratching my head. Wyatt Angstrom was like a multitude of entertainment types that sift through Los Angeles. I didn't know him well, but I knew his kind. They uncovered opportunities, built relationships, and self-promoted exceedingly well. Their relationships with women were more often designed to advance their careers than to find a soul mate. It was obvious he didn't care much about Amanda Zeal; maybe he had good reason. And since I didn't have a next move lined up, I did the thing that I always did when I had an hour to kill. Find coffee.

A studio commissary is unlike that of most corporate lunchrooms. There are salad bars, pasta bars, sandwich bars and smoothie bars. There are frozen yogurt machines, with an astonishing number of toppings. There is something for almost everyone. As we had not yet moved past breakfast, they also had a muffin selection that extended beyond most imaginations, and bagels said to have been flown in daily from New York. The coffee stand offered ground beans from multiple countries, and today was featuring a cup of outrageously priced coffee made with beans from a brand called Jamaica Blue Mountain. Studios did what they could to keep employees happy. If anyone asked why a movie ticket in L.A. cost almost twenty dollars, here was one possible reason.

"How is that Jamaica Blue?" I asked a gorgeous young

woman wearing a green apron with the Fox TV logo in the center. The *barista* had shiny auburn hair that tumbled in waves halfway down her back, and displayed a smile that was big and bright and flashy. She looked all of twenty years old, but she also looked like she might have been a contestant in a recent Miss Teen USA contest. I didn't bother to ask if she was an aspiring actress. Some things are just too laughingly obvious.

"People say it's fantastic," she said, but added, "I can't speak from experience though. I only drink green tea."

"Ah. Is this Jamaica Blue worth, let's see here, eleven dollars a cup?"

She smiled again and playfully shrugged. I had no great desire to impress her as a big spender, and even less desire to part with eleven dollars for coffee that might taste remarkably ordinary.

"Well," I said. "I think I'll just take the house blend."

She turned toward the back counter, ground some beans, and did a pour-over, which is little more than sloshing hot water over the coffee and waiting for the mixture to sift through a filter and slowly drip, drip, drip into a cup. The process took about four minutes and cost me three dollars. I sat down at a table by myself, took a pleasant sip, and decided no coffee was worth eleven dollars unless it also came bundled with a full breakfast.

After an hour of combing through my iPad apps, I had learned about what was going on in the world, or at least the world I cared about. The Rams were favored to win their conference championship game on Sunday, Congress was threatening to shut down the government again, and the weather forecast for the next week in L.A. was balmy and warm. At that point, I stowed my device, paid another three dollars for a second cup of house blend, and tried to not let the gorgeous *barista* notice I was ogling her. The gold ring on my left hand reminded me to not mess up the very good thing I had. So, I sat back down and did some people-watching. The time went by quickly. Grady Pinn arrived at exactly eleven o'clock, wearing a button-down oxford cloth shirt, tailored slacks, and cordovan loafers.

"Oh my word, it's the Trojan warrior!" he exclaimed, his southern-tinged voice as silky smooth as thirty-year-old bourbon. "Don't you get up my friend, you look remarkably comfortable."

I took his advice and remained seated while I shook his hand. It was a warm handshake. Everything about Grady Pinn was classy and effortless. In his fifties, he had a head full of distinguished-looking silver hair, and a permanent tan. He was pleasant to look at and effortless to listen to. Grady was the type of person the gods probably conjured up when they were contemplating how to best construct middle-aged human beings. From an outsider's view, he had an idyllic life and a career many would kill for. I got the feeling traffic lights turned green for him whenever he drove down the street.

"Thank you for meeting me, Grady. I appreciate it."

"Not a problem, my friend. I do appreciate, over the past few years, your taking time to speak with me before our broadcasts. You helped me make those USC games better. I'm no football expert, but I learned a lot about how to defend against a jet sweep and a bubble screen."

I smiled. "It's mostly about getting the defense in the right position. And knocking people down."

"Well, you helped me lend some authenticity to the broadcasts. And I got props from my color man, too. Former football players love it when you can throw around terms like a single high safety or shooting the A-gap. Made me sound like I knew what I was talking about."

"Happy to help. You still make the broadcasts fun to listen to. That golden voice."

"Sure," he said. "So, tell me what brings you to the studio today. I heard you went back into law enforcement. When Johnny Cleary left for the Bears. Don't tell me you're looking at another career change."

"Nope," I said. "I have no interest in being a sportscaster."

"Good. This business has far too many amateurs. Mostly former jocks who can't speak proper English, or talking heads who won't put in the time to learn the game. It's a tough world to break into, and a tougher one to do well. A few of us make it look easy, so anyone thinks they can pick up a mike and call a game on TV."

"That's somewhat related to why I wanted to talk to you. Tangentially, perhaps."

"Tangentially? Another word I'll remember. Well, please go on."

"Amanda Zeal. I know you worked with her. She was part of your crew covering Pac-12 college games this year."

In an instant, Grady Pinn's pleasant expression flipped to something that looked painful. "Yes, she was on our team," he groaned.

"Not sounding like you had a positive experience."

"Look," he managed. "The networks all hire these sideline reporters now. The girls are eye candy. I get it. It drives viewership to have a sexy woman in front of a camera. And they're often able to buttonhole a coach at halftime and make them want to spend thirty seconds talking about how their team has to stay focused, work harder, blah, blah, blah. But that's the main purpose. Get viewers to stay on the channel and watch them. Most of those girls are just two-legged cupcakes."

"And Amanda ... ?"

"She was a treat to look at. And her voice was getting better. But look, you can't harangue coaches in the middle of the game."

"Harangue?"

"Yes. Harangue. Or maybe accost. She would get in a coach's face and press him on why his team wasn't performing better. Try and pin him down on specifics of what they were planning to do in the second half. No coach in his right mind is going to give up his strategy in front of a TV audience. And they don't appreciate being badgered."

"Anyone at the network try and tell her this?"

"*Ad nauseam*, my friend, but it was like talking to the wall. She was stubborn as a mule. No give in her. But things finally got bad at the Rose Bowl a few weeks ago. I'm sure you remember that game."

I did. It was a marvelous day, and one I'd remember for a long time. I met Johnny Cleary and his wife there, and I was able to bring Marcus along. USC beat Michigan that day, and after the game, we went down onto the field and my five-year-old son got to meet some of the players. He did a high-five with the USC quarterback, Patrick O'Malley, and was still glowing from the experience.

"I certainly do recall that one. But what happened with Amanda?"

"She started going after the Michigan coach, and some of their fans overheard her yelling at him as their team came out of the tunnel at halftime. Some fans took exception. Mostly some jawing back and forth. But one fan jumped out of the stands and had to be physically restrained. They gave him a security escort out of the stadium, but that's the type of emotion she evokes in people. And it's not a good thing."

"Yes," I agreed, scratching my head. "Then why is she still on air? Like you said, there's lots of people trying to get into the business. Replacing her couldn't be hard."

"Harder than you might think. She's connected. Someone in management at the Fox network likes her. Might be a boyfriend, who knows. But when our producer tried to make a change, the word came down from up top. She stays. The network thinks she has spunk and adds spice to the broadcast."

I nodded. "Helps to have friends in high places."

"Or learn to go low," he responded dryly, before catching himself. "Listen, it's the same as when people complained about Howard Cosell back in the day. Or Skip Bayless now. They annoy a lot of viewers, but the viewers tune in to hear them. It becomes must-see TV. What kind of outrageous comment would they utter next. It's all about getting eyeballs."

"Show biz," I concurred, and then followed up with the paramount issue, the one I came to inquire about. "She get any threats?"

Grady Pinn gave me an odd look. "Funny you should ask. Is that why you're here?"

"It is."

He pushed his tongue against the inside of his cheek, seemingly being deep in thought. It was an actor's technique, used by people who wanted to give off the impression of deep thinking, but it was also employed by people considering just how to phrase a response in the most delicate of ways.

"We all get threats, you know. Comes with the territory. Criticize a fan's favorite team and there's always some goofball out there who'll be furious. It's almost always bluster. Nonsense, and usually nothing comes of it. The worries I have are from the guy that gets mad and *doesn't* contact us. But the threats we get are typically empty ones. Meaningless."

"But Amanda's gotten them."

Grady sighed. "Yes. And more than a few. If you watch her on the sidelines, you'll see some burly guys nearby. Added security. As I said, a few fans have gotten into it with her, mostly yelling, and the network likes the heckling. But they're aware it might evolve into something more."

"You say that *usually* nothing comes of these threats. That's not so reassuring."

"No, it's not. And our team just wants to do a broadcast. No one wants to get caught up in anything beyond that. Do our jobs, cash our paychecks, and go home."

"You think these threats are just from fans venting?"

"Pretty much," he said, standing up to signal our time had come to an end. "But we're talking about human beings here.

And this is America. You can't rule anything out."

"Thanks. This is helpful. Appreciate your taking the time."

"Not a problem, but I have an eleven-thirty meeting with the crew that's broadcasting the Rams game on Sunday. They're aware I know a thing or two about that Goff kid; he used to play up at Cal."

I smiled. "In three years, he never beat USC. Our defense shut him down."

"Right. I called a couple of those games. Your boy Johnny Cleary should have taken my advice and stayed at SC. He's making a lot of money in Chicago with the Bears. But eventually he'll get fired, because almost all NFL coaches get fired. And as you know, college is special."

"I agree."

"And," he added, casting a more-than-casual glance at the beautiful *barista* who made my coffee, "you can't top the women on a college campus. Although a studio lot comes mighty close. I call those girls a side benefit."

"I call them a walking lawsuit."

"Well, you know, I like living on the edge."

"Careful, Grady," I warned, feeling oddly paternal as I watched my comely *barista*. "Some of these girls are young enough to be your daughter."

He smiled. "I'm fifty-five, but I feel twenty-one."

"Uh-huh," I said. "If that were true, I'd wonder what you were doing at twenty-one."

Grady Pinn threw back his head and laughed, clapped me on the back, and headed toward the exit. I finished the final bit of my coffee, walked over to the garage, and drove my Pathfinder back out into the real world. I sailed down Pico for a short while, and then I saw the sign for the Apple Pan and decided now would be a good time for lunch. It was early enough to grab a seat at the counter without waiting, and I was rewarded with one of life's simple but wonderful pleasures. The Apple Pan had been around for over a century. It maintained that old-style charm but still served a hickory burger that was second to none. I had been coming here since I was five years old, and the joint had never changed. I thought about the Amanda Zeal case, and how I was learning a lot but not coming up with good answers. But on the way back to my car, my phone rang, and something on this case changed, and changed dramatically.

"This is Burnside," I said.

"Mr. Burnside," came a voice that sounded very familiar, but one I couldn't quite place right away.

"That's me. Who are you?"

"This is Detective Slick. Beverly Hills PD. Haven't spoken with you in what, a day now?"

"Of course. How have you been all this time?"

"I'm all right. Can't say the same thing for the corpse I'm looking at right now."

"Oh?" I said warily. "Somehow I'm connected to them. Man or woman?"

"Well, that's pretty obvious, let me tell you. Don't need to be a detective to figure that one out. But whoever killed Anthony Machado shot him in the head four times at close range. I'm calling you because we found your phone number on his recent call list. We also found your business card inside his pocket. Any idea how it got there?"

Four

Amanda Zeal's apartment building was two blocks off of Beverly Drive, in an ornate, well-designed, and well-maintained building that had a white exterior with curved, black metallic trim on the entryway door. There was subterranean parking, protected by a long gate that had been left conspicuously open. There were six black-and-white police cruisers parked outside, and there was yellow crime scene tape set up across the garage entrance. I ducked under it as I walked down into the garage.

Detective Drew Slick was dressed in a dark gray suit and sported a stylish green-and-blue striped tie. He had an unblemished face and a calm demeanor, with his blond hair parted on the side and combed back. He had blue eyes and a square jaw, and could have easily come out of central casting. It had been half a dozen years since I had last seen him, but he looked remarkably the same, and that was oddly reassuring because Drew Slick looked exactly like what a Beverly Hills detective should look like. But he was still a cop, and there was no mistaking the jaded expression on his face. In some detectives, the look is more world-weary. But that was LAPD. This was Beverly Hills, and it came with a touch of sophistication.

"Burnside," he said, giving me the once-over. "Thanks for coming over so quickly. I always appreciate it when the private sector does what I ask them to do."

I smiled a phony smile. "Whatever you like, Detective. I'm here to help."

"Well, that puts my mind at ease," he replied, pointing to a white sheet covering what was once a very large human being. It was about thirty feet away. "This is Mr. Anthony Machado. What I'd like you to help me with is how Mr. Machado came to have your card in his pocket and have your phone number on his call list. That's the extent of what we have to go on."

"That's it?"

"That's it. Right now, all we've got is some stiff who lived in a downtown slum, and came out here to get shot in the head. Oh yeah, and we've got you. Maybe you can fill in some details for us."

"I'll do the best I can."

"Sure. Maybe go above and beyond, eh?" he said, pulling out a small notebook and clicking the top of a blue gel pen. "How'd this Machado guy come to know you?"

"We went to high school together."

"Go way back, huh?"

"Yeah, but until yesterday, I hadn't seen him since then. I got hired by Phil Zellis, owns a home here in Beverly Hills. You know about his daughter, Amanda Zeal, getting attacked the other night. Guess it happened down the street from here. Phil wanted me to look into it. And he wanted Anthony Machado, who, by the way, we nicknamed Moose, to protect Amanda."

Drew Slick turned and pointed to the sheet on the ground. "Didn't do his job real well, now, did he?"

I gave him the palms up sign. "Can't really tell," I said. "Maybe he took a bullet for her."

He pondered this for a moment and then moved on. "Okay. Just how are all these people related? This Machado, Amanda Zeal, and Phil Zellis?"

"Phil Zellis is Amanda Zeal's father. She changed her name. Works as a sideline reporter for Fox, doing college football games. Phil, Moose and I all played football together. Culver City. About a million years ago."

"Oh, yeah?" he remarked, suddenly more interested. "You were a football player in college, if I remember."

"I was."

"Me, too. I used to play football at UC Davis. Quarterback. But my playing days were probably a lot more recent."

I felt my hand balling into a fist. "And my playing days were with a school most football fans have heard of."

Slick chuckled. "We weren't Alabama."

"You weren't even Utah State."

"Uh-huh," he said. "So, what do you make of that assault the other night?"

"Funny, I was going to ask you the same thing."

"Don't get cute. I read the report. Pretty skimpy. Amanda Zeal and this boyfriend get attacked out of nowhere and then the thugs take off. Not a lot to go on."

"The thugs left in a rented white van. They think it might have been from Star Rentals."

"Oh?" Drew Slick said, eyebrows raised. "Didn't see that in the police report. What else you uncover? This is starting to get interesting."

I stopped and wondered just how interesting the days of a Beverly Hills police detective normally were. I sensed the answer was not very. In wealthy communities, the main crimes center mostly around home burglaries, with the occasional domestic assault popping up, when some man with more money than sense decides to take out his minimal frustrations in life by slapping his wife around. The opportunity to tackle a murder case should be one that makes a detective salivate.

"Amanda's boyfriend is named Wyatt Angstrom. Works over at Fox. I saw him this morning. He had a few marks on his face. And his eyes were red from pepper spray. Supposedly it got on him accidentally."

"Accidentally?"

I shrugged. "Said he must have gotten some on his hands during the tussle. Fighting off the bad guys."

"You believe in accidents?"

"Nope," I said, thinking neither did Sigmund Freud.

"Okay, so we got the two thugs from the other night, and we've got the boyfriend, the father, and we got you. Anyone else we need to mix in?"

"Not yet. But there's Amanda's grandfather. Used to be on the job, Largo Beach PD."

"Former cop, huh? Okay. Means he's almost certain to have access to a firearm. What's his name?"

"Ed Zellis. I understand he still lives in Culver City."

"Right," he said, and closed his notebook. "Again, what do you make of this? Girl and her boyfriend get assaulted by a couple of perps, the dad hires some muscle to protect her, and the muscle goes and gets himself whacked. And the girl's not around afterward."

"Maybe someone didn't want the muscle around. Maybe whoever did it was after Amanda. Maybe she got away and went into hiding. Lots of maybes."

Drew Slick stared at me for a minute and then walked over to a uniformed officer, who listened to him and then walked into the building. He returned about fifteen minutes later and said something quietly into Slick's ear. The Detective talked to another officer before he made his way back to me.

"She's not in her apartment. My guy just ran into a neighbor who said he saw Amanda and Machado leave the apartment together around ten-fifteen, a couple of hours ago. Makes sense. This got called in by someone who found the body a few minutes later. Let me ask you something. Were those two a thing, do you know? They hook up?"

I was mildly impressed. "What I heard is they had some sort of a relationship. Goes back a few years."

Slick nodded enthusiastically. "Oh yeah, that makes sense. Jealousy, disputes, grudges, this is starting to add up. You say her boyfriend works for Fox? Wyatt Angstrom?"

"Yeah, although I wouldn't be that quick to judge. I left his office a little before ten o'clock. And it doesn't explain the guys in the white van."

"Nope, it sure don't. And no one's seen a white van here today. We'll check the cameras to be sure. But it's possible to leave Fox a few minutes before ten and still get here at a quarter after. In fact, the timing is exceptionally good. He could have arrived right when they were coming downstairs."

"Maybe so," I acknowledged.

"And I'm not ruling out the dad and the grandpa. What's the dad like? He got a temper?"

I thought about how to respond. I clearly remembered Phil Zellis and his anger issues, ones that dated back to high school and probably well beyond that. He had little control over his temper, but back then, teenagers settled disagreements with their fists if they couldn't talk them through. Nowadays a lot of people have guns, and the stakes have risen accordingly. But Phil was the one who brought Moose on, so it made no sense for him to go and shoot him in the head a few days later. But a lot of things about this case were making no sense.

"I don't know. It's been a long time since I last saw him."

"Okay," Drew Slick said. "Anything else you can tell me about this Machado guy?"

"He owed money to some bookie. Goes by the name of Mike White. Not sure if it's a real name. I don't know if that helps, but it probably doesn't hurt."

"Got any contact info?"

I wrote down the phone number Moose gave me and handed it to him.

"Good," he said. "What else do you know about dad, this Phil Zellis? You think he knew about Machado and his girl?"

"He never said, but probably not. If he did, he wouldn't have brought Moose on to look out for his daughter."

"Uh-huh. So, the dad's a homeowner in Beverly Hills. But

the grandfather's a retired cop who lives in Culver City, where you guys grew up. Tell me how that happened."

I smiled. "The son made his money the old-fashioned way."

"How's that?"

"He married into it."

Drew Slick gave a small snort of laughter. "Ain't that the American dream? Okay, we got a bunch of suspects now. Let's see where this goes."

I wondered if I should add that we might also have a missing young woman, Amanda Zeal, who was observed heading down into the garage with the victim, but was mysteriously not around after he was killed. There was no sure sign that she was missing; no one had seen her being taken against her will.

"I guess you've got it all handled," I managed.

"Yup. Good leads. Thanks, Burnside. I'm surprised. For a P.I., you've been a lot more helpful than I imagined."

"Let's just say I find this kind of work interesting," I said, not feeling especially helpful any longer.

Detective Slick gave me a long look. "Okay. Like I said, we've got some suspects to delve into."

"You forgot one."

"Oh yeah? Who?"

I gave him a long look this time. "Amanda Zeal."

*

The afternoon sun shined brightly as I walked out of the subterranean garage. The crack Beverly Hills police force would be investigating the death of Moose Machado, and they were unlikely to require the services of a local private investigator. In fact, they would undoubtedly prefer my not poking around in their business. There was no law against my investigating this crime, but neither was there any substantive payoff. There was however, the glaring issue, the one I was indeed being paid for. Uncovering why Amanda and Wyatt were attacked, and just who had attacked them. That Amanda herself seemed to have disappeared into the wind made this already cumbersome issue even more taxing.

Hopping back into my Pathfinder, I pulled out my iPad and scanned the internet for the address of Phil Zellis. I decided the time was ripe for an in-home visit with my client. Phil and Joy Zellis lived on Coldwater Canyon Drive, in a house that was worth more than I would likely earn in two lifetimes. I studied the photos of their home, nicely provided by a realtor who had listed the property a few years ago and kept it on his website for reasons that went no further than self-promotion. The Zellis's home was a 9-bedroom, 6-bath monstrosity that probably housed just two people these days, but looked as if it could accommodate a dozen more, and easily at that.

Cruising up Beverly Drive, I sailed past a variety of expensive jewelry stores, art galleries, and fragrance shops. The streets turned residential after seven or eight blocks, with gorgeous, stately manors quietly sitting along the ostentatiously wide street. The distinguishing part of Beverly Drive was not the remarkable homes, but the long rows of palm trees, exceedingly tall, bending unevenly toward the western sun, their signature sharp leaves jutting out at the top. I drove slowly through a pair of six-way intersections, where three streets crossed. In some cities they built roundabouts to deal with this oddity, which allows drivers to easily move from one street to another. In Beverly Hills they did no such thing. Getting through a six-way intersection requires a certain amount of patience and a certain amount of politeness. It was a little after two o'clock and the traffic was light, so the drivers were cooperative. I imagined trying to sift through this strange impediment during rush hour, a chore which might easily deteriorate into a festival of honking horns and extended fingers. But a Beverly Hills police officer once told me that these intersections actually had the fewest number of accidents in the city. Go figure.

The huge Zellis home was a gray, two-story structure, with blue trim around the windows and half a dozen alabaster columns lining the front. A thick series of perfectly manicured green hedges framed the property. There was a narrow driveway, along with a front entrance that featured a steel gate. I parked and walked up to the entrance. The gate was locked, hardly a surprise for Beverly Hills, but I caught the attention of a gardener near the side of the property, wheeling a lawnmower. What was a surprise was that he came right over, smiled, greeted me in English, and let me in.

It took a good thirty seconds to walk to the front door, and after pressing the doorbell, it took another thirty seconds before a young woman in her mid-20s flung the door open. She had shoulder-length blonde hair that had both the color and consistency of parched straw, along with large brown eyes and pink cheeks. She was tall and buxom, pretty in the way a stripper might be pretty. She had a wide mouth and perfect teeth.

"May I help you?"

"Yes, my name is Burnside," I said and handed her my card. "Is Phil available?"

"Phil's not here," she responded, looking down at my card carefully.

"Will he be back soon?"

She didn't answer immediately; rather, she kept eyeballing my card and trying to assess something. Finally, she looked back up at me. "Are you the person Phil hired?"

"That's me. I knew Phil from high school. Culver City."

"Yes, right, he mentioned it. I'm Joy, Phil's wife. Oh, come in, he should be back in a few minutes," she said, opening up the door and inviting me inside.

Their house was marvelous. The foyer had a muted gray-and-white tile floor, with a tall atrium that held a sparkling crystal chandelier. There was a circular staircase and a number of hallways that branched off in a few directions. Some colorful artwork lined the walls, and I slowly drank it in as Joy Zellis led me into a large living room. There were two plush couches facing each other, a number of easy chairs, and a white baby-grand piano in the corner. The tall glass windows looked out on a large green backyard, with a pool, a Jacuzzi and a cabana.

"Phil out running an errand?" I asked casually, as I sat down in one of the easy chairs.

"No, he was playing the back nine at Riviera. He finished a little while ago, which means he should be home anytime now."

"Ah."

"Can I get you something to drink?"

"No thanks, I'm good."

We sat in silence for an awkward moment before she spoke again. "Have you, um, found out anything about Amanda?"

"No," I said, trying to deflect. "In fact, I probably have more questions now than I did when I started."

"Like what?"

I paused. "We should probably wait for Phil."

"Yes, of course," she said, and we endured another long silence before she spoke again. "I guess you and Phil go way back."

"We do. High school. Are you from L.A.?"

"No," she replied. "New York. I came out here to break into acting."

"How's that going?" I asked, knowing the likely answer.

"It's tough. When a girl hits a certain age, the roles dry up."

I didn't bother to point out that she barely looked over twenty-five, and that there was probably a fifty-fifty chance she was younger than her step-daughter. Instead, I just agreed with her.

"Show business is a tough racket," I said, then asked the question I was most curious about. "How did you and Phil meet?"

"Oh, I was temping a couple of years ago. The agency sent me to Phil's office. It was love at first sight."

"I'll bet."

"I know what you're thinking."

"No, you probably don't."

Her mouth opened and closed, and then we heard the bang of a door being slammed. The molecules in the room seemed to shift immediately, from an awkward space where neither of us knew quite what to say, to an anticipation of Phil's entrance. Joy rose and walked across the room as Phil entered. She greeted him with a full mouth kiss that lasted a beat too long. He patted her on the butt and walked over to me. I felt like I was in a bad movie.

"Burnside," he said, shaking my hand. "You didn't need to come over. Unless something's happened."

"Something has," I said, and made a motion with my eyes, that Phil, surprisingly astute, picked up on. He turned to his young wife and asked if he could be alone for a few minutes with his old friend. Joy's mouth didn't open and close this time; rather, it curled up and she sucked in a deep breath. Turning on her heels, she left in a huff, shutting the door loudly behind her. Phil turned back to me, sighed, and sat down on the couch.

"Sorry about that," he said. "We're having some problems."

I looked at him and didn't say anything.

"So, what's happened? You find out who went after Amanda the other night?"

"No."

Phil frowned. "What is it, then?"

"It's Moose. Someone shot him in the garage of Amanda's building. He's dead."

The news caught him off guard, and his body swayed backward, as if he had been hit with a gust of wind. He gazed off into the distance, confused. Finally, he refocused and turned back to me.

"Good Lord. What happened?" he asked.

"All we know is that Moose was seen accompanying Amanda this morning at about ten-fifteen. A neighbor saw them leave her apartment and head down the elevator. That's about it right now. The police will review the footage from any video cameras."

"Is Amanda all right?"

I looked down. "We don't know. She wasn't there when the police arrived."

"Oh, God," he said quickly.

"Look, Phil. Try not to overreact to this."

Phil reached into his pocket and jerked out a cell phone. He tapped a few buttons and placed it to his ear. I could hear the endless ringing and I could see the increasing desperation in Phil's eyes. The ringing turned into voice mail, and Phil left a brief message imploring his daughter to call him immediately. He slapped the phone down on a glass coffee table.

"I have no idea what to do," he managed.

"She could have simply left the scene unharmed. Where might she have gone?"

"I don't know. Maybe to her brother's apartment, Aaron's place. He lives down at USC. Maybe to Wyatt's. As long as Wyatt wasn't involved in this."

"You think he was?" I asked.

"I don't know. But I do know, well, he has a past."

"Really? Like what?"

"I had someone look into his background. It's complicated."

It certainly sounded complicated, and it sounded downright murky that Phil Zellis had hired me and then not bothered to disclose this part of the story. This was not completely unusual. People hire private investigators to do a certain task, and they are often stingy with the details, be it due to shame or privacy or the need to maintain control of the information flow. It made my job harder, and it delayed getting clients resolution of their issue.

"The more I know, the more I can help you."

Phil glanced at me, but it was hard to see if he comprehended this. "Not much I can say at this point."

"Okay. Here's the thing. I need to ask you a few questions. Were you aware of anything going on between Amanda and Moose."

His head shot up and he looked me dead in the eye. "What do you mean?"

"You know what I mean."

Phil shook his head. "He was like an uncle to her. Maybe a big brother. That's all."

"But they were close."

"Get your mind out of the gutter. My daughter would have never touched Moose. And if I knew he tried anything with her, I would have killed the bastard."

I put up a hand. "Whoa. Stop. Look, the police are going to be here soon. You need to think about this. And you need to compose yourself. I can dismiss remarks like that because I know you. You make those kinds of comments around the police, you're going to get yourself in a jam. Do you understand what I'm saying?"

He didn't respond, so I sat there and let that sink in. There was a part of me that wanted to help him, and a part that wanted to learn more about what Phil knew and what he didn't know. But there was a fine line that separated Phil from being a client and being a suspect. If Phil had anything to do with Moose's demise, I couldn't let it go. But if he was just a bystander, he didn't need to put himself in harm's way.

"Can you help me here?" he finally asked.

"Sure. What do you want me to do?"

"You can start by trying to find Amanda."

I nodded. "Okay," I said. "But I'll need your son's contact info. As well as any friends of Amanda's. And if you've received any threats, I need to look at them or listen to them."

Phil said okay. I said okay. I wondered if I should suggest to Phil that he have a conversation with a criminal defense attorney. I wondered what was going on behind the scenes. I wondered if Moose was targeted or if he just got in the way. This case was indeed getting interesting. Maybe too interesting.

Five

The untidy relationship between Moose Machado, Amanda Zeal, and Phil Zellis was both confusing and intriguing. There were a lot of unanswered questions. Phil hadn't provided many details, Amanda had disappeared, and Moose would not be available for comments going forward. I started thinking about who might have some hidden knowledge about their situation, and two people sprang to mind. One was our former football coach at Culver High, Frank Fultz. But Coach Fultz lived inconveniently far away, in a small town outside of Palm Springs. My phone call to him was picked up by his wife, who said he was unavailable all day. She did not tell me anything further. The other person who might add something to this was Phil's first wife, Suzy Zellis, who I learned through Facebook, now goes by Suzy Barber. She also lived in Beverly Hills, albeit on the wrong side of Sunset Boulevard.

It seems a contradiction in terms to refer to a tony neighborhood containing large, beautiful homes as the poor section of Beverly Hills. There is no poverty in Beverly Hills. There are no homeless, the streets are swept, and the lawns are manicured. There are often flower beds on the paths leading up to the front door, and the exteriors are elegant and stately no matter what street you're on. It is as close to a model community as one could conjure up, a series of well-maintained homes which cradle both the haves and have-mores. Most of Beverly Hills can be accurately categorized as gorgeous; it's just that some parts are just more gorgeous than others.

Suzy Barber lived in a spacious house on Almont Drive, a few blocks north of Olympic, and not too far from Amanda Zeal's apartment. It was an older art deco-style home, the exterior featuring some very large windows, which allowed pools of light to pour in. The rooms on the second floor had small balconies on them. The house went well back into the property, and a white Mercedes sat in the driveway. Unlike her ex-husband's digs, there was no security gate, and no impediment to my simply strolling up to the front door and ringing the bell.

I heard a woman call out that she would be a minute, that she was on the phone, and to please wait. I waited for what was probably three minutes before the door, made from what seemed like an expensive form of distressed wood, opened. A woman in her mid-forties stood there, blonde, very pretty, with a few lines on her face. She wore faded jeans, torn at the knees, and a black, long-sleeve top. Both were covered with drips of various colored paint. Oddly, it did not look bad on her. She gave me the once over, and said nothing, waiting expectantly for me to begin the conversation.

"Hello. Are you Suzy Barber?"

"I am. And who might you be?"

"My name's Burnside," I said, handing her my card. "I'm a private investigator."

She scrutinized the card. "Apparently you are. It says so right here. What can I do for you?"

"May I come in?"

"No, you may not," she said matter-of-factly. "Despite your impressive credentials, I really don't know who you are. And I'm not in the habit of inviting men I don't know into my home."

"I understand," I said, and it was clear I had to make myself better known to her. "Actually, I was hired by your ex-husband, Phil. We used to play football together in Culver City. That was before he moved on to Vassar. I gather the two of you met there. And then you had Amanda. And then Aaron. And then Phil took over the plastics company your grandfather founded. And then sold a few years ago before you two got divorced."

Suzy Barber stared at me for about five long seconds, but she no longer seemed to harbor expectations of me to say anything. Without a word, and as if in a stupor, she stepped back and motioned me inside of her home. I walked into a small living room, nicely appointed, but far from the ostentatious surroundings of her former husband. The hardwood floors were made of bleached oak, and some incomprehensible art hung on the walls. I sat down on a curved-back pine chair with a red seat cushion. It looked as if it would be uncomfortable, but surprisingly, it was not.

"I apologize for the intrusion," I said. "But I did need to

speak with you. I'm not sure how much you communicate with your ex these days."

"We move in different circles," she acknowledged, leaning against an archway a few feet from me.

"Okay," I said. "I get it."

"So, were you and Phil old friends? He never mentioned you."

"We took different paths," I told her. "I stayed with football and then moved back and forth, in and out of law enforcement. Honestly, until the other day, I hadn't spoken to Phil since our high school graduation."

"Why did he hire you?" she asked.

"It's about Amanda. She was assaulted a few nights ago near her apartment. Phil wanted me to find out what happened."

Staring at me as she tried to comprehend this, she finally spoke. "Is she all right?" she finally managed.

"Amanda wasn't injured badly in the attack. She carried some pepper spray with her."

Suzy gave a smirk. "Phil probably gave it to her. Sounds like something he would do."

"He did. I take it you haven't spoken to your daughter about this."

"My daughter and I aren't close. In fact, we're somewhat estranged. We grew farther apart after the divorce. It's like she chose whose side to be on."

"Oh?"

She lowered her eyes. "I had Amanda when I was very young. Too young. I was just twenty years old and a sophomore in college. I tried to go to classes and take care of her, but that just wasn't possible. So I stayed home with her. Phil was the one who got his degree."

I watched her carefully. "Sounds like there's a little resentment there."

"There's a lot of resentment there. Having a child turned my life upside down. I dreamed of being an artist when I was younger. It finally happened, but it took over twenty years for me to become the person I wanted to be."

"That must have been difficult," I said as sympathetically as I could, recognizing I was sounding like an amateur psychologist.

"It was extremely difficult, especially at first. I knew nothing about being a mother, but I knew I didn't want an abortion. I thought this all might work out. But, as I said, I was just twenty and I didn't know what I was getting myself into. Amanda was a difficult baby, colicky, always getting into things when she was a toddler. She never really grew out of being a problem. She was always testing limits, and Phil let her get away with too much. She began hanging out with the wrong crowd as a teenager, drinking, drugs, the whole bit. I probably bear some responsibility, but again, there was a lot of resentment toward her. In the end, I think I just said if she wants to ruin her life, go ahead. Be my guest."

I took this in. "Do you know anyone who might have wanted to harm her?"

Suzy sighed. "Most every boy she ever went out with. She was a tease and a flirt. I imagined this behavior might go away when she became an adult, but perhaps not."

"Any names you can provide?"

She shrugged. "I can try and remember a few, but I'm sure

they're years in the past. I doubt they've interacted with her lately."

"But if Amanda were to need a place to stay, who might she contact? Close girlfriends? Other family?"

"Aaron, I would imagine, over at USC. Her brother seemed to get along with her for some reason. She didn't have a lot of girls who were friends. A few, but most moved out of L.A."

"Okay," I said, as a dozen questions floated through my mind. I considered the reality of being curious, and the curse of being an ongoing student of human nature. It meant that scratching that itch often led to being incredibly nosy. "And what happened between you and Phil? I know you're obviously divorced. But how is it you two wound up where you are?"

"You mean why is he living in a mansion north of Sunset, and I'm living here?"

"This place doesn't seem that bad."

"No," she replied. "I suppose it's not. But it's all relative. So to speak. Phil ended up running my family's business. He did a good job, he has a head for that sort of thing. I don't. Never did, never will. I'm an artist, and I could never begin to make heads or tails out of a financial statement. But Phil pulled some nasty stuff when he was running the company. Not exactly illegal, but unethical as hell."

I frowned. "Such as?"

"Phil set up a number of what my attorney called shell companies. They were partly designed to shield money from the IRS, but mostly designed to put that cash straight into Phil's pockets. When we got divorced, around the same time we sold the company, there turned out to be a lot of cash missing. I hired forensic accountants to try and make sense of it all. They said it might take years to unravel everything, and the cost of doing this would be exorbitant. In the end we reached a settlement. We both walked away with a lot of money. He just got more of it than I did. It was as if he had it all planned."

"That must have made you pretty mad. Your family's business and all," I pondered, watching her carefully.

"Of course it did. And after a few years in therapy, I've come to grips with it. I have it good, better than most. I live in the house I grew up in, I love my neighbors, and I've built a studio in the back. My daughter and I have had a falling out, but I'm close to my son. Life isn't perfect, but it's not bad now."

"And it was bad before, because of the divorce...?"

"The divorce, sure. But even before that, the lying, the cheating, the running around with other women. My friends would tell me about it, but, well, I had two kids to raise, so I turned a blind eye. I shouldn't have, but I did. You know, people envy you when you have money, but it doesn't protect you from some very painful things in life. Then one day I said I'd had enough. I was just finished with the marriage. The kids were old enough to deal with their parents separating."

"And that's when you asked for a divorce."

"I didn't ask for anything, Mr. Burnside. I told him we were done, I told him what I thought of him, and I told him he'd be hearing from my attorney. He responded the only way men like Phil respond to conflict. With violence. After he hit me, he spent a week in jail, and it probably taught him a few things. It also taught me something about my daughter. Amanda largely stopped speaking to me. She couldn't believe I would do that to her father."

I took this in. "Was Phil violent with you before this?"

She looked out the window for a while, and responded without turning back to face me. It was almost as if I weren't even there.

"Not with me. But Phil was a tough guy. He got into a lot of fights in college. If a guy started talking to me at a party, he would step in and give him the evil eye. He was a bully, I'm sure you knew about this part of Phil, you had to, I'm certain it didn't start in college. Given his background, it wasn't a surprise. In the beginning I liked the security of having someone strong near me. Over time, it became a burden. But through therapy, I also realized he is the way he is because of how he was raised. His father was one tough bastard. Phil's behavior just mirrored his dad's behavior."

"One can easily surmise that," I said, "the apple doesn't fall far from the tree."

"That is more true than you might imagine."

"Interesting comment. What do you mean?"

"Ed lives in quite a nice house, up atop Culver Crest. It's especially nice for a civil servant," she said. "Maybe too nice."

I had been wondering about this too, although I reminded myself that police officers get paid more than most government employees. They put their lives on the line, and there was always the grim realization that each day might be their last. It was not something cops thought about much, but it was a reality most had in the backs of their minds. The above-average pay helped justify their career choice, almost as much as wielding power over anyone who challenged them.

"You think there's something unsavory going on with Phil's father?" I asked.

"It always struck me as so. And, well, Phil has a lot in common with Ed," she mused. "I'd say Ed taught him well, they both ended up with nice houses and big bank accounts, but I wouldn't say either is living a happy life. You've met Phil's new wife?"

"You mean Joy? Yes, I met wife number two today, in fact."

"Actually Joy is wife number three. Number two lasted about a year. I don't know how long he'll be with Joy, but she's cut from the same cloth as the last one. Young, pretty, and she has dollar signs in her eyes. Phil's going to be spending a lot of his fortune on alimony. At least with me it was a cash settlement. We split and went our separate ways."

"And how did the kids take all of this?" I asked.

She looked troubled. "Well, Aaron doesn't like that his dad is hitting on a younger generation of women. Amanda is on better terms with them. Phil's new wives are practically her peers. They'd go shopping together, go out for cocktails. It's a little strange to see the step-mom who's only a couple of years older than my daughter, but welcome to our world."

"This is interesting," I admitted, although this line of inquiry didn't seem to be getting me any closer to finding out what happened to Amanda Zeal, or where she might be. It did seem to be okay with Suzy Barber; she seemed oddly at peace talking about what could have been a difficult subject. Maybe a few years of therapy had really done some good.

"So, were you aware of Amanda's relationship with an Anthony Machado?"

"You mean Moose," she smirked. "I knew. I found out a few years ago, a friend's mother told me. But she was in college by then, and technically an adult, so she could do what she wanted to do. I told her she was being foolish getting involved with a brute like that. She could do much better. But it was a strange relationship, they would see each other for a while, then stop, then start up again."

"Why do you think she went out with him?"

"It's like I said before, Mr. Burnside. There is something secure about being with a man who is physically strong. That's something my daughter and I have in common. That, and we've made some poor choices in the men we've gotten involved with."

*

Suzy Barber's comment about Ed Zellis and his extra-nice house got me interested. I looked up his address and drove over to Culver Crest, a small hillside community overlooking much of the Westside, still technically part of Culver City. I parked on a narrow street in front of a home that might best be described as mid-century modern. This meant it was built in the 1950s, but it hadn't been updated, and as such, it maintained the curious charm of being old but still fashionable. The home was long, with redwood siding on the exterior, and a sharply angled roof. When I was growing up, a house like this might have cost about a hundred thousand dollars, which was high-end in those days. Today, a home like this would sell for over two million.

I rang the doorbell and waited a minute until the low, muted shuffling sounds in the distance turned into louder, more noticeable shuffling sounds nearby. The door opened, and a ruddy looking man of about seventy years old faced me. His gray hair was cropped short, but he still had a lean, hard torso, and ice-blue eyes that likely didn't miss much.

"Help you?" he barked.

"You're Ed Zellis?" I started.

"Uh-huh. And you're not."

"The name's Burnside," I said, stifling a desire to shake my head, and handing him my private investigator card. No sense flashing my fake badge to an ex-cop. "We've actually met before. I went to high school with Phil. We played football together."

"Burnside, Burnside," he said, looking up at the sky, as if that would jog his memory. "Name doesn't ring a bell, but okay, maybe you did. What can I do you for?"

"Okay if I come in?"

"Nope. State your business here. Be quick about it, too."

I looked at him. Ex-cops are not the most trusting of souls, and I really couldn't blame them. There are plenty of scam artists around, and they often prey on the elderly, although I pitied any grafter who tried to con Ed Zellis out of his money. He appeared as if he could still handle himself well.

"Phil hired me to look into what happened to Amanda a couple of nights ago. I'd just like to ask you a couple of questions."

"Something happened to my granddaughter? What's that? She lose one of her diamond earrings at a Hollywood party?"

"No," I said carefully, "a couple of guys tried to attack her and her boyfriend outside of her apartment in Beverly Hills. They didn't do much damage, but Phil wants me to look into it."

He glowered at me, looking incredulous. "What the hell'd my son hire you for? Should have gone to the cops or called me. I spent twenty years as a detective down in Largo. I was a real detective with a gold shield. He didn't have to bring in some private joker like you."

I sighed and took a look beyond him into the interior of his home. It was a nice home. It was the type of home that a doctor or lawyer or corporate executive might live in. It did not look like the home of a retired public servant, even one that worked down at Largo Beach, a large port city on the border of Orange County. But there had long been unsavory rumors about the Largo Beach Police Department. I started to give the rumors more credence.

"I spent thirteen years with the LAPD," I said slowly. "Worked plainclothes for a long time, although I never got that gold shield. Maybe it was easier to get down in Largo. But now I'm out on my own. So I'm hardly a private joker. It's not like I did tax returns before I hung out a shingle."

"You were LAPD?" he squinted at me.

"I was."

"What division?"

"Bunch of them. Mostly Broadway Division, down by 77th Street. Also worked vice up in North Hollywood. My captain there was Pete Bates. You may have heard of him, he's Chief of Police now."

Ed Zellis stared at me. "Oh, yeah, I've heard of him. Know

him, too. Better than you might think. Lives just over in Baldwin Hills. They call that the black Beverly Hills now. I call it something else."

I didn't bother to ask what Ed Zellis called it, and didn't really want to know. Baldwin Hills was next to Culver Crest, and was like a number of nearby communities, including Fox Hills, Windsor Hills, and View Park. Previously all-white neighborhoods before the 1960s, the ethnic makeup rapidly changed when a few African-American families moved in. Many residents quickly put their homes up for sale, fled the area, gutted the property values, and helped bring the phrase "white flight" into our lexicon. In less than a decade, the demographics shifted dramatically. But now, these communities had actually completed a metamorphosis, changing from mostly white to mostly African-American, then to a regentrified mish-mosh that was something in-between.

"How do you know Chief Bates?" I asked.

"Played poker with him over the years. A few ex-cops get together, plus we got a former running back from UCLA and a couple of college football referees, too. It's a good group, lots of stories, lots of laughs. Bates got invited one week, friend of a friend. Stayed on. Probably one of the few places he could just be himself, you know, public figure and all. I've made a lot of money off of him. Good police chief, but a lousy bluffer. Anyways, I know Pete ran North Hollywood back in the day, okay, you sound legit. If you're not, I got a .44 in my pocket."

"Thanks for the heads up."

"Just letting you know. Well, you seem all right, so come

on in," he said as he opened the door. I walked into a neat and well-decorated home, if well-decorated also meant the style was stuck in the 1960s. The carpet was an orange shag, and the furniture was narrow and colorful. But the view would never go out of style. The far living room wall was all glass and provided a good glimpse of the L.A. basin. As I got closer, I noticed it was actually a great glimpse. You could spend an afternoon just staring out at that glimpse. I sat down on a burgundy recliner that creaked when I leaned back and was probably as old as the house. Like everything else here, except for Ed, it seemed to fit the motif remarkably well.

"Nice place," I said. "Must have cost you a bundle."

Zellis gave me a curious once-over. "Let's just say I did well in the stock market."

I nodded and took a glimpse out the window again. It was tough to take my eyes off of the view. Then Ed Zellis barked at me again.

"Tell me what happened to my granddaughter," he demanded, taking a seat in a rocking chair across from me, but not bothering to rock. The chair seemed odd when someone was sitting in it without rocking, but everything seemed odd in here.

"Pair of guys jumped out of a van near her apartment building. They assaulted her and her boyfriend, Wyatt, although they fought them off. No money taken. But she may have been targeted."

"Targeted, huh? More like that jackass boyfriend of hers was targeted. Never liked that guy. Worked for a movie studio. Never trusted those Hollywood types."

"Your daughter works for the same employer," I offered.

"That's different," he sneered.

"Why don't you like her boyfriend? I mean, aside from him being in show biz and all."

"He's under investigation for some shady deals, he has a rap sheet. Guy's a real crook, I thought that from the beginning."

I frowned. "How do you know he's being investigated?"

Ed Zellis stared at me like I was an idiot. "I just told you I play poker with the chief. You ought to listen closer."

"I ought to do a lot of things," I pointed out. "So you asked the chief to look into Wyatt. As a favor?"

"Yeah. Sure. As a favor. I tried to warn Amanda, but kids, you know," he said, his voice trailing off.

"You think this incident might have been related to her boyfriend, not her."

"That's where I'd start," he said, his mouth curling. "If I was investigating this matter. Which I'm not. But I ought to be."

"Anything more you can tell me about this Wyatt?"

"I'd check out his bank account. See if he's made any recent purchases, like a new car. Renewed his passport. That kind of thing."

I didn't bother to respond. In addition to not working for the LAPD any more, there were only so many favors I could call in from friends like Juan Saavedra, and only so many tickets to Lakers' games I could provide. Ed Zellis seemed to have forgotten neither of us still worked for police departments, and neither had access to any records. I thought of telling him what happened to Moose Machado this morning, and that Amanda might be missing. But there was something about Ed's demeanor that told me he might not handle that information in a rational way.

"So," I said, changing the subject for a moment. "How long have you been retired from Largo PD?"

"About ten years. Wound up being on the job almost thirty-five. I was the longest-serving cop. Except for the chief. Top brass always stays on a long time."

"Long time," I observed.

"Had an injury at the end. Messed up my hip. After a while, I figured it was time to hang 'em up."

"You figured that, or the department told you to go?"

Zellis continued to give me the once-over, although he seemed a bit more defensive and less curious now. "Don't you worry about how that played out. Bottom line is I served that community well. It was a better place because I was there."

I didn't see any point in arguing with him. And I knew certain police and fire departments had instituted what some called a deferred retirement program, mainly designed to allow veteran officers to stay on the job longer. Unfortunately, there was a component that also allowed officers to take extended leave due to job-related injuries. At full salary. So there were a lot of aging cops who collected a paycheck without ever showing up to work. Some managed to game the system for years. One cop even claimed bad knees due to an on-the-job accident and then started a scuba-diving school while he was recuperating from surgery. I knew of a few LAPD officers who had abused the system, and when they were caught, they simply retired and began collecting a hefty pension. The program, like many others, started out with good intentions but quickly fell apart when unethical people found easy workarounds to game the system.

"So, you were a detective," I said. "What'd you work on?"

"Narcotics," he said, with a measure of pride. "Port of Largo Beach is a major smuggling point. Lots of contraband coming through. Used to be mostly coke back in the day. Now it's all sorts of things. None of them good."

"You ever work vice?" I asked, wondering if we had anything in common.

"Yeah, but not for long. Hated it. Mostly dealing with perverts. I liked busting drug dealers. Drugs are the worst thing to ever be perpetrated on America. Everything bad that's happened to this country, you can tie it back to drugs. Messes up lots of lives. I made a difference. Kept it out of the hands of some kids."

"Okay," I said, not entirely sure of where this was going, but at least Ed Zellis was talking to me. "What else do you think you can tell me about Amanda? If it wasn't about her boyfriend, is there any reason why anyone else would want to hurt her?"

Zellis shrugged. "Hard to say. Lots of crazy people in the world. Believe me, I've met a lot of them. They watch TV and think the person on the screen is talking to them. They aren't. But go tell them that."

"Okay. But you were on the job once. If you were looking for Amanda, where would you start?"

"I'd start with people close to her," he said. "Not her parents, though. Maybe her little brother. It's not hard to disappear into a college campus for a little while. All them kids look the same."

*

I arrived home just as Gail and Marcus were sitting down to what looked like a hearty dinner of spaghetti and meat sauce. A place-setting was there for me, but the empty plate told me they were hungry, and had not been optimistic about my arrival. They were, in fact, going to start eating with or without me.

"Daddy!" Marcus yelled. He put his fork down and ran over and gave me a hug. This was my favorite part of the day. Gail followed and did the same.

"I didn't know if you were going to make it," Gail said.

"Oh, ye of little faith. I arrived in the nick of time," I responded, then sat down and began helping myself to dinner. "How was everyone's day?"

"I did a slam dunk today!" Marcus exclaimed.

"Oh?" I exclaimed, pretending wonder for a brief moment. "That's exciting. But it also sounds like a bit of a tall tale to me, Marcus."

"They were playing on a three-foot hoop," Gail pointed out as she twirled some pasta onto her fork, using her spoon as a base, a trick I taught her years ago.

"Daddy, where am I going to school next year?" he asked.

I glanced over at Gail, but she continued to focus on twirling her pasta. I turned back to Marcus.

"That's an interesting question. Why do you ask that?"

"Brendan said he's going to ... the Cross school?"

"Crossroads," Gail added, looking up. "Brendan's older brother is going there, that means he should get accepted because he's a sibling."

"What's a sibling, Mommy?"

"It's when you have a brother or sister," she said.

"Am I going to have a brother or sister?"

Gail looked at me and then looked down again. "We don't know, sweetie. Sometimes you get them. Not always."

"Daddy, did you have sib ... what was that again?"

"Siblings," I said. "And no, I didn't. I was like you, Marcus. I was an only child."

"Did you like that?"

I stopped for a moment. I hadn't told Marcus much about my formative years; they were difficult years, ones I didn't enjoy reliving. My father died in a car accident before I was born, and my mother raised me as a single mom. I never recalled her dating anyone. It was just the two of us. She said she liked it that way. I missed out on having a dad, and she sometimes struggled with money, but my mother made sure I didn't lack for attention. And I found a number of male role models along the way; some were terrific, some were not.

"Being an only child," I said, "came with some challenges. I had a lot of friends in my neighborhood, but no, I didn't have a brother or sister. Might have been nice, but then I'd have had to share my mom with someone. I wouldn't have minded. It just would have been different."

Marcus took this in and then changed the subject to when we would be going to Disneyland. Fortunately, he didn't bring up the issue of schools again. It was a topic Gail and I needed to discuss, frequently put off, and was not the type of conversation we wanted to have in front of our five-year-old. After dinner, Marcus went off to play a video game, and we did the dishes together.

"How was your day?" I asked.

"All right," she said. "I have a new case. A ring of car thieves. They've discovered a low-tech way to steal cars that doesn't require any tools or weapons."

"Sounds intriguing. How do they do it?"

"They walk around a neighborhood at night, preferably a nice one, an area that has newer cars around. They try the door handles, and inevitably they find a few that are unlocked. What's interesting is that some people leave a spare key inside their car. Or their bedroom window is close to the driveway where their car is, so the fob keys are nearby. Most new cars have fobs, so all the thief has to do is push the starter button. If it starts, they simply drive away, no muss, no fuss. If the car doesn't start, they simply ransack the interior, pop the trunk and take whatever they can."

"Ingenious in its simplicity," I said. "How'd they get caught?"

"A neighbor was just getting home from a night of working late. He saw it happen and followed the car, called it in to 9-1-1 and the LAPD nabbed them."

"And the thieves aren't copping a plea?"

"They claim they're doing a public service by alerting everyone to this issue. They say it's all for the greater good. And this was their first offense."

"We live in strange times," I observed.

"And how was *your* day?" she asked.

"Not the best," I answered. "Did you hear about Anthony

Machado?"

"No. Wasn't that one of the guys you went to high school with? That friend of Phil Zellis?"

"If you can call them friends. Anyway, Machado was the one Phil hired to protect his daughter. They found his body in the garage of her building. Gunshot wounds to the head."

"Oh my," she said. "No, I hadn't heard that. If it happens outside the city limits, we usually hear about it the same way everyone else does. Lead story on the ten o'clock news."

"Yeah. So Machado is dead, and the daughter is missing. No idea where she is. Phil asked me to find her. I've been talking with her family and with her boyfriend, but so far I've got nothing. *Nada*."

"I'm sure you'll get an idea of where to look."

"Maybe. Anything else going on?"

"Well, I got some surprising news. Shane Karp is running for City Attorney. It was announced today by his campaign committee."

"He has a campaign committee already?" I asked.

"It's part of the process. Mostly for fundraising and P.R."

I thought about this. While we had nibbled around the edges of the topic, Gail and I had not discussed the nuts and bolts, the gnarly specifics of her running for public office. We'd have to explain to Marcus what it would mean if his mother ran for an important, demanding, and highly visible position. The City Attorney of Los Angeles was a big job, and it would take some money to get there. Campaign contributions would need to be sought, and there were donors who would need to be wooed. And it was not uncommon for candidates to take out personal loans or use their home equity when borrowing money. It was often why a lot of those who run for public office already enjoy a significant level of wealth.

"What else is included in this process?" I asked.

"Mostly gathering signatures to be on the ballot, to start. Then filing, then campaigning. For positions that are lower-profile than mayor, a lot of the push comes right before the vote. Mailers mostly. TV advertising isn't normally done for City Attorney campaigns, it's too expensive. But even mailers cost a lot of money, especially in a city this big."

"Sounds like that requires quite a large bit of money."

"It does. But it often gets raised through holding fundraisers, and calling big donors for contributions. I wouldn't use any of our money, we're not rich. I'd have to work something out. And if this became a problem for you or me or us, I would just stop."

"Okay," I said. "When you say right before the vote, I assume that means right before the primary."

"Yes. L.A. is a deep-blue city. Whoever wins the Democratic primary in the Spring is typically going to win the general election in November."

"Good thing you're a Democrat."

Gail stifled a grin and leaned against me. "I know you're not."

"Yup. My independent streak crosses over into politics. Although if you run, I might consider giving up my values and joining a party."

"That's so romantic."

"Thank you."

"So sweetie, you're aware I never ask you who you vote

for. Lord knows, couples have enough things to fight about. But I'm curious about something. When you were doing work a few years ago for Rex Palmer, did you vote for him for governor? He's a Republican, as I'm sure you recall."

"I have no idea."

"Excuse me?" she asked, eyes wide. "You don't know who you voted for?"

"Nope."

"You mean you don't remember who you voted for," she said, clarifying.

"No. I honestly didn't know who I voted for. Still don't."

"Take me through all that, would you?"

"Look," I said, "I didn't really see the difference between Rex Palmer and Justin Woo. The ballots are just a punch card with a lot of numbers on them. You use a pen to fill in the circles of the candidates you want. Kind of like taking the SATs. You know. You pick number five if you want Palmer, number six if you want Woo. Maybe it was the other way around. I don't know."

"So you didn't bother looking into who you voted for? You might as well have not voted at all, then. For you, it was the equivalent of a coin toss."

"Yup. And that's how I feel about most elections. The lesser of two evils, normally."

"Then why bother even voting?"

"It's my civic duty," I smiled.

"Okay, enough of this. Listen. I have a lot of things to think about. Shane Karp is a good man and a good prosecutor, but I don't think he's the best choice to lead our office. And he's not great with people."

"If you think you'll be better, you should run."

"Okay. But you have to be all in on this," she said.

"I'll support you in anything you want. My concern is that my past may come up and hurt your chances. Not everything I do in my job is savory. I don't want you to get affected."

"I'm a big girl. And if I worry about people criticizing me for my personal life, then I shouldn't get into politics. But are *you* okay with me being under public scrutiny?"

I stopped for a moment and considered this. I recognized I would be able to handle seeing myself under the microscope; it was something I had gone through before and could go through again. I had become somewhat anesthetized to other people's opinions of me. But I also knew it would be far easier for me to deal with a harsh public spotlight than it would be to see Gail put under that lens. It is one thing to endure hardships yourself; it is quite another to sit by and watch someone you love have to go through that same torturous process.

"I'll do whatever you want," I said.

"Thank you, sweetie," she said, wiping her hands on a cloth and turning to give me a big hug.

"Would you like me to do some opposition research on Shane Karp?" I whispered.

She laughed. "No. At least not yet."

"Should I do some oppo research on you?"

Gail stepped back and gave me a long look. "You know, that is a very good idea."

"I was kidding," I said.

"I'm not," she countered. "If there's anything in my past that I've forgotten about, be it some silly photo during high school, or some paper I wrote in college, yes, I'd like to see if you can find it. Because I'd rather have you find it and have a response ready, than to get caught flat-footed."

"Okay," I said and made a mental note to do some opposition research on the beautiful Gail Pepper. And I made another note to do some on Shane Karp.

Six

Xavier Bishop called me back just as I was crawling under the covers to go to sleep, so I suggested we talk in the morning. He told me to swing by his house in Baldwin Hills when I got up. I asked how early I could come, and he told me to stop by whenever I felt like it. He said he was an early riser.

Baldwin Hills is populated by, among others, a variety of athletes and former athletes, successful doctors and lawyers, and a sprinkling of movie stars. Mayor Tom Bradley used to live there, as did Ray Charles and Tina Turner. The homes were nice, the views amazing, and many streets boasted teardowns-in-progress, where perfectly livable homes were purchased, leveled, and rebuilt to two or three times their former size. It was no different than other upscale communities in L.A., except that for many decades the residents here had been primarily African-American.

Xavier's home was off of Don Felipe Drive, not far from La Brea. I needed to navigate up a narrow hill, one that seemed to go on and on. I wondered if I would motor through a cloud. The properties on the street were nice, but when I reached Xavier's, I knew I had arrived at someplace truly special. His home was hidden behind an ivy-covered stone wall, with sprigs of red bougainvillea crowning the top of it. I needed to double-check the address with Google maps to make sure I was actually at the right place, since there were no street numbers on the property.

The driveway was blocked by a large opaque gate, with a security phone nearby. I pushed a button, and without a word, the gate swung open a few seconds later. I did note a discreetly placed camera perched on top of the wall, one that obviously captured anyone attempting to gain access. Parking next to a cherry red Ferrari, I took a long look at it before walking to the front door and knocking. The door opened a few seconds later, and I was treated to a sweaty, muscular Xavier Bishop, wearing a red, white, and blue Buffalo Bills t-shirt and dark nylon pants. He was grinning and he gave me a warm handshake.

"Not going to give you a hug right now my friend," he smiled. "Just finished my morning workout."

"I appreciate your consideration, X," I said, looking around. "Nice crib you've got here."

"Let me show you something," he said, the grin on his face not going away, and he led me past a living room overloaded with too much black leather and smoked glass. We walked onto the back patio. "While I've still got this place."

"Still got it? You miss some mortgage payments?"

"Nah. I'm just thinking of moving. There's been some break-ins down the street. I want to live in a safe neighborhood."

I understood. Break-ins could happen anywhere, and a swank neighborhood like this attracted its share. Baldwin Hills was a nice area, lined with expensive homes. The mostly well-off professionals who lived here were law-abiding citizens and they normally had good kids. But my police work many years ago taught me these good kids sometimes had friends from outside the area who weren't so good. They drove up here to hang out, saw a lot of nice homes, residents at work during the day, and envisioned a grand opportunity for monetary gain. Many burglaries happen in the middle of the day, and a surprising number were committed by these casual friends of their neighbors' kids. There were simply more items of value to steal here than in their own neighborhoods.

"Makes sense," I finally said. "You've done all right in the NFL. You can afford to live where you want."

"Yeah. Plus, I'm a free agent this winter, which means I'm going to be making monopoly money soon. Gonna move on up. Maybe Beverly Hills. Think I'll fit in?"

I laughed. "If you've got the money, you can fit in anywhere. In L.A., the most important color is green."

Xavier's backyard was worth showing off. The sparkling pool and steaming Jacuzzi were ringed by a series of small date palm trees that looked as if they had just been planted. A teak fence lined the perimeter, but the crown jewel was the view, an imposing, spectacular look at the L.A. basin, one that put Ed Zellis's vista to shame. I would imagine however, that as expensive as Ed Zellis's house was, Xavier paid a lot more money for his place.

"I got to look at who my next team should be. I'll make top dollar, but I got my legacy to think about now."

"Legacy, huh?" I said, and gave him a playful poke in the ribs. His abdomen was as hard as stone. Xavier Bishop was a USC cornerback I had never coached, but I did help him out of a jam a few years ago. Falsely accused of beating his then-girlfriend, Desiree, Xavier faced suspension from the team and possible expulsion from school. And a pro football career that was hanging by a thread. I was able to find out that someone else had hit Desiree, and I convinced her not to ruin Xavier's life because of a falling out they recently had. Xavier became a first-round draft pick for the Buffalo Bills and had excelled at the next level.

"It's all about getting me a ring, now," he smiled, and invited me to sit down on one of the chaise lounge chairs surrounding the pool. The chair was comfortable and the view was nice. All I needed now was a cup of Starbucks.

"You'll have your pick of teams," I said. "Pro Bowl cornerbacks are in big demand. You coming back to play in L.A.? Can't beat the weather in December."

Xavier shook his head. "The Rams are set at corner. And the Chargers aren't going anywhere. I'm not concerned about the city, I'll spend six months a year here in L.A. That's enough. Got a lot of family and friends nearby, but when it's time to work, I want to focus. Can't get distracted."

"Buffalo was probably good for that."

"Oh, I don't know," he laughed. "You can get in trouble anywhere, but it's true there's less options in western New York, let me tell you. Anyways, it's time to move on. I'm thinking Kansas City, New Orleans, maybe Dallas. Want to go to a contender. I've been in the league for five years now, and I've only been in one playoff game. You don't play forever. Got to get what you can while you can."

"True," I said, impressed at how Xavier had turned out. Not every athlete takes a long view; some think they'll play for fifteen years. A few will, but it's mostly happenstance. Being a pro football star has a short shelf life, and players have to make their money and get paid quickly. They never know when a freak injury will end a career.

"You said something about needing my help," Xavier said. "After you got me out of that mess with Desiree, I'll help you do whatever."

"Good to know," I said, hoping I wouldn't need any whatever. "You used to be involved with a girl named Amanda Zeal. Or so I've read on the internet."

"Oh, man," he said, throwing his head back. "Don't remind me of that one."

"What happened there?"

"Met her in a club last spring. Over in Hollywood. Went out a few times, but she was just a little too much. Used to getting her way, bossing guys around. That don't work with me. Don't work with most men."

"So nothing came of it?"

"Just a fling, man. Just a fling."

"I've heard she's been involved with a few other players."

"Wouldn't surprise me. Girl look like that. Football players are young, rich and we're in great shape. And we like to have fun. She was a little different from the others, though."

"In what way?"

"Seemed very impressed with my money. Maybe they

don't pay her well at Fox. Went crazy over my Ferrari. I see that with lots of girls. But you don't expect it from girls that grew up in Beverly Hills. You know what I'm saying?"

I said I did, even though I didn't fully understand. "Anything else?"

Xavier shrugged. "Once you get past the party girl stuff, it struck me she was a little messed up inside. Don't know what the problem was. A couple of months ago she called me and said something about her family having money problems, and wondered about getting a loan from me. I joked with her and asked if her family was mobbed up, and she didn't laugh. Something there, but I wasn't about to pry."

"Okay. Any other players she might have been involved with? Anyone who might have had a problem with her?"

Xavier scrunched up his mouth. "Yeah, you know, in fact I do. And he lives in L.A., he's with the Rams now. Name's Rhett McCann. Played with him a couple years ago when he was with the Bills, plays nose guard. He got traded to the Rams right at the end of training camp last summer. Worked out great for him, they're still in the tournament. Next playoff game's on Sunday."

"You think she just had a fling with him, too?"

"I don't know, but it got nasty. She went into her act with him, trying to be a tough girl, I don't think it ended well. That's the rumor anyway. But I learned my lesson, you never put your hands on a woman. Learned that with Desiree years ago. So for me, I just walked away from Amanda. Right out the door. With Rhett, sounded like things got weird."

"How so?"

"I think he might have hit her. Least that's what someone

said. No video, no police report, so no proof. It never got out, so the league never stepped in. But I heard he was pretty mad at her about something."

"What do you think set him off?" I asked.

Xavier raised his hands upward. "Could be anything. Some women just get off on drama. With Amanda, she was flirting all the time, always after something. Plus, the money thing. That stuff gets old."

"Okay. Tell me about Rhett. Nose guard. Must be a big guy."

"Big just scratches the surface. Dude weighs about three-forty. Thing is, he's quick, too. Not fast, just quick."

"Is he from L.A.?" I asked.

"Nah, and maybe that's part of the problem. He's from a small town in Texas, or someplace like that. They got some hot girls in Texas, hell, there's hot girls everywhere if you know where to look. But not many of them do men like this."

"Rhett have a temper?"

"He's a grown man. And a football player. And he plays on defense. So yeah. What's your guess?"

It didn't take much for me to conjure up a scenario. Football players are aggressive by nature, and defensive football players take that up a notch. Angry guys, the ones with the chips on their shoulders, naturally gravitated to defense. It was almost in their blood. The other team's offense is trying to move the ball, which takes a lot of scheming; the defense tries to stop them, which takes a lot of fury. I knew something about playing on defense, that was my side of the ball, and I recognized anger comes with the territory. I carried my share of anger, too.

"Let me ask you this. If I told you someone was stalking Amanda Zeal, would you believe it?"

"Sure. Hot girl like that, oh yeah."

"If I told you someone tried to assault her on the street, would you believe that?"

"Yup. Girl be crazy. Nothing would surprise me. Hey, you know what else I remember? She told me she tried to change her last name to Zzyzx. Can you believe that? Must have really wanted to get attention."

"Zzyzx?" I asked.

"Yeah, that's that place on the way to Vegas? Everyone driving from L.A. to Vegas seen it."

It was indeed true there was a Zzyzx in the Mojave Desert, right near the Nevada border. An ex-partner on the LAPD told me his grandfather had once gone there for treatment of an injury. Legend has it that Zzyzx began as a health spa, founded by a doctor who went on to become a minister. He was said to have discovered what he claimed were natural hot springs, a divine cure-all for nearly every sort of malady, from sore feet to cancer. He called it Zzyzx because he wanted it to be the last word in health care. In the end, the founder was revealed to be neither a doctor nor a minister, and his natural hot springs were little more than a series of man-made ponds heated by a boiler. His cures relieved nothing, except money from the pockets of unsuspecting marks. The founder ultimately went to jail, and his Zzyzx creation became little more than a curiosity, a strangely memorable freeway signpost for Angelenos headed to and from Las Vegas.

"I guess the name didn't get approved," I said, wondering

why anyone would ever want to change their name to something associated with a con artist.

"Nope. Someone at Fox straightened her out. Got her to just change her name to Zeal. But who even thinks of doing that? Like I said. Girl be crazy. The thing about it, though, she brings out the crazy in a lot of men."

"Then what do you think actually went down with Amanda and Rhett?"

"Can't say that he hit her or didn't hit her. And I don't want to cast aspersions."

"Aspersions?" I peered at him.

"Yeah," he smiled. "My new favorite word. My agent's an attorney. Really smart dude, I think you know him. I'm picking lots of things up. Trying to improve myself."

"But getting back to Rhett," I said, trying to refocus him. "You might not rule out him being involved in something violent here?"

"Can't say. But I will tell you this. All of us have hangers-on. Friends of friends that want to get close to us. Do us favors so they can hang with us. I get it. Comes with the territory. I have to be careful what I say and who's around when I say it. If I'm mad at someone, one of these guys may go, hey, I'll take care of that person for you. Try to get into your inner circle. Sometimes they don't even tell you until afterward. That's how it works. Again, no idea if Rhett's involved. But that's just how it is."

"You know how I might contact Rhett?" I asked.

Xavier nodded slowly. "I'll call him and set something up. He'll meet with you. But don't let on I told you everything. That wouldn't go down well."

"No problem."

"You know, I wouldn't do this for most people. Heck, I don't think I would do it for almost anyone else, outside of family. But you helped me out of a big problem a few years ago. I owe you big time. I wouldn't be where I am today if it weren't for you. That's the truth. Any way I can help you, I'll do it. Want to rob a bank? I'll drive the getaway car."

I smiled. "It won't come to that. But I do appreciate your help. And I'm glad I was able to get you out of that mess with Desiree. Speaking of which, do you ever hear from her?"

Xavier smiled back. "Oh man, do I ever. In fact, she's sleeping upstairs."

"You're kidding."

"Nope. We worked out our stuff. And guess what? We're going to be parents in about four months. Ain't that something? Wouldn't have happened without you. I'd probably be in jail and she'd be living in a one-bedroom apartment along Crenshaw. You changed the course of human events."

I took in a breath and managed to congratulate him. I thought of telling him if he was going to have a stable family he'd need to stay away from sideline reporters like Amanda, and away from girls like that in general. But some things weren't exactly my business. And I figured Xavier knew what the right thing to do was. Actually doing it was the hard part.

*

I began driving back down the hill toward La Brea when my phone started buzzing. The area code seemed familiar but I couldn't place it. Hoping it wasn't another telemarketing call trying to sell me on solar panels, I tentatively pushed the speaker button.

"Burnside."

"Well, that's a name I haven't heard spoken a while," boomed a familiar, gravelly voice on the other end.

"Coach Fultz!" I said loudly, resisting an urge to jump up and stand at attention.

"Who'd you think it was?" he demanded. "You called me, I'm calling you back."

I chuckled. Coach Fultz had been leading the Culver City High football team for over four decades before he retired a few years back. He was almost seventy-five when he stepped down, and he hadn't lost his edge. His decision to hand over the coaching reins was more to give his longtime assistant an opportunity to coach for a few years, not because he was losing anything. He had said at his farewell dinner that he felt he could coach winning teams until he was a hundred, and there were a few of us who thought he just might be able to pull that off. He often said age is a state of mind, and when one of his former players jokingly asked him what it was like to be old, the coach replied that he'd let him know one day when he found out.

"Coach, it's good to hear your voice."

"I'm sure it is. I was wondering what happened to you. Coaching over there at USC one moment, then Johnny Cleary leaves and you disappear. You get out of coaching?"

"I did. Loved the players, hated the hours. Wanted to see my son grow up."

"All right," he said. "I'll let you slide on that one. How

old's your son?"

"He just turned five."

"Gonna be a football player?"

"I don't know, Coach," I started, "that would be fine by me. But my wife's got other ideas. She's concerned about concussions."

"Your wife's a smart cookie. I wrote all that concussion stuff off, but I'll tell you, the doctors are coming back with proof now. I think they're right. Hate to say it, because I love all that hitting that goes on. I didn't personally see any of my kids get hurt, but the problems are showing up later in life. I see it out here in Palm Springs, some guys in my bowling league are having memory issues. A lot of them played in high school. I'll tell you, football's going to be a different game in a few years."

"You may be right," I said.

"Of course I'm right. And you listen to that little wife of yours. Women are smarter than men, you know that, don't you?"

I smiled. "Yup, I do."

"Good. Everything going okay with you back in L.A.?"

I paused. "For me, things are fine. I'm back to being a private investigator. I'm actually working on a case for Phil Zellis. Remember him?"

"Of course I do. Private eye, huh? Oh, I'll bet you're good at that. You were one of the smart ones. You and Phil, couldn't believe my good luck to have you two studs on my defense that year. The year we went to the title game."

"That was a great season," I concurred. It was our senior year, and we had gone undefeated the whole year, won three straight playoff games and went to the city championship game at the Coliseum. Little did I know that would become my home for the next four years in college. We played Dorsey and it was one tough game. It was late November, and it was drizzling the entire day. Dorsey had the lead 14-13 with two minutes to go, but we were driving down the field. On a first-down play on the Dorsey twenty, our quarterback faded back to throw but was overwhelmed by the pass rush, got strip-sacked and Dorsey recovered the fumble. We never got the ball back, and they won the game.

"You boys did well. I always said that was the best team I ever coached."

"Sorry we couldn't bring home a ring for you, Coach."

"Now, you remember what I told you after the game?"

I did. Coach Fultz borrowed a line from Vince Lombardi and said we didn't lose that day, the clock just ran out on us. It was exactly the type of line Coach loved to use. In the beginning of the year he said he didn't care if we lost all of our games, as long as we played hard and never gave up. And he added that if we always played hard, good things were bound to happen. Coach Fultz was tough as nails, but more than fair in a lot of ways. He told us to never complain about a referee call, no matter if they were dead wrong, and to also never castigate a teammate for a loss. We won as a team, we lost as a team. He taught us to avoid being put in the position of having to try and win a game in the last minute, because anything can happen on one play to affect the outcome. He said with our talent we should always be ahead by three touchdowns in the fourth quarter. He would rail at us during the week, but on game day he was a happy warrior, cheering us on, patting us on the helmet after a good play, telling us to put our mistakes behind us and not focus on them. As a teenager, Frank Fultz was the closest thing I had to a decent father figure.

"Coach, I remember everything you taught us."

"Good. But it sounds like you didn't call just to reminisce."

"No, and I'm sorry, but I have some bad news."

"What?"

"It's the Moose. He passed away. Tragically, I'm afraid. Someone shot him."

"Oh my God," he said. "I'm sorry to hear that. Real sorry. Deep down, Moose was a good guy. But you know, I can't say as I'm totally shocked."

I blinked as I steered onto La Brea and headed toward the 10 freeway. "How so, Coach? You stay in touch with Moose?"

"No, but I stay in touch with a few players. A few of the dads, too. Funny you should bring up Phil. His dad, Ed, is one of the fellas I kept up with. He'd always be at our games. Called me up during the season to talk football. But he also kept up with a few of the guys on your team that year. Guess Moose had a rough life. Maybe he's in a better place now."

"Why do you say that?" I asked.

"Ed told me Moose was heavy into gambling. Had some losses. Went and asked Ed for a loan."

"What did Ed do?"

'Well, Ed isn't the kind of guy who gets all mushy. I guess he told Moose to go face his problems like a man. Not sure I would have been that tough on him."

"You think his gambling debt might have something to do with Moose's getting shot?"

"Can't say for sure. And it doesn't quite make sense to me. If the wise guys wanted their money, it seems that shooting Moose wasn't going to get them that."

"You know," I said, trying to piece all of this together, "Moose was hired by Phil to look after his daughter, Amanda."

"Oh yeah, I see her all the time on TV. A real cutie. You say she needed looking after? How come?"

"Someone tried to assault Amanda the other night. Phil asked me to look into what happened," I said, realizing I hadn't exactly been doing a bang-up job myself. "Ed ever mention his granddaughter?"

"Oh sure. He was proud as heck of her. Phil, too. Ed was glad they didn't have to do what he did."

I frowned. "How's that? You mean police work?"

"Yeah. You know about Largo PD. Crooked cops and all."

"I heard the rumors over the years," I said. "Was Ed involved in this?"

"You seen that house he lives in now?"

"Yes."

"Then you know the answer."

"Hey, Coach," I broke in. "How do you know this?"

There was a small pause. "A couple of my other kids had dads that worked Largo PD. I heard things. No one in your class, it was a few years after you graduated. I had to suspend one of the kids from the team when he was caught with some coke. Learned he found it at home, the dad was a cop, he had taken it off of some drug dealers. I heard cops sometimes use that stuff as payment to snitches. Maybe they took some extra on top of that. You'd know better than I would. But something didn't smell right."

"Yeah," I said, wondering if that's how Ed financed their nice lifestyle growing up. The vacations, the nice cars, the private college tuition at Vassar. All handled through dad, which meant it was paid for through some means other than a civil servant's paycheck. I also wondered how Phil would have turned out if he hadn't wound up going to college at an exclusive school. He wouldn't have met his first wife, the daughter of a Beverly Hills tycoon, he wouldn't have ended up taking over a multimillion-dollar business, and he might have had more of a hardscrabble existence.

"Coach, can you tell me who the dad was? I'll promise to keep your name out of it. You won't have a problem."

There was a brief silence, then an exhale of breath. "All right. His name's Bart Sokolov. And don't worry about me. I can still handle myself."

I jotted the name down. "Thanks Coach, I appreciate it. And I'm sorry I had to tell you about Moose."

"Yeah, well, I hope you can catch the scum who did this."

"We're working on it," I said, making a note to call Detective Slick for an update. "How are you doing, otherwise? Life good in Palm Springs?"

There was a long pause. "I'm getting by."

"Just getting by? Coach, I have to tell you. You sound pretty spry. The wife told me you were busy all yesterday."

"Thanks, but the reality is I was getting an infusion yesterday."

"Oh no."

"Yeah. I've been getting chemo treatment. Prostate cancer. The doc puts me on steroids for a few days around the time I get infused. Takes some of the sting out of pumping toxin through your body. I like to joke the steroids are adding muscle, but you know the side effect is I have a ton of energy during this period. I'm so wired, I go on a five mile run. No joke. But once I stop with the steroids, I crash and sleep for a few days. It's tough, but I'm managing."

I hated to hear that. In addition to feeling badly for Coach Fultz, this brought back some sad memories of when my mother had been diagnosed with lung cancer. She chose not to go onto chemo. As a nurse, she had seen firsthand what cancer patients often had to go through, and she wanted no part of it. She elected to try and tough it out, but cancer is not always a winnable battle, and it wasn't in her case.

"Coach, I'm really sorry to hear you're going through this. I truly am."

"Listen son, I've had a good life. I'm almost eighty. You take what life throws at you and you make the best of it. I'm not complaining, not feeling sorry for myself, and neither should you."

"Okay."

"And I follow that old line."

"What's that?" I asked.

"First thing I do when I wake up is I go outside and get the newspaper. Then I check the obituary page. If I'm not in there, I go and eat breakfast."

*

The Rams' practice facility was across the Ventura County line in Thousand Oaks, but fortunately Rhett McCann lived a little closer to me, in Calabasas. This was an upscale bedroom community nestled in a canyon area on the western edge of the San Fernando Valley. He confirmed Xavier had just called him and said I was okay, and he could meet me before practice. He suggested a Jamba Juice outlet in a strip mall. Fortunately, there was a Starbucks a few blocks away, so I arrived with my steaming cup of *grande* Sumatra.

Rhett McCann was a big man to say the least. Xavier's estimate of three-hundred and forty pounds might have been on the low side. He was huge in every way, from his big head with curly reddish-brown hair to his massive arms to his enormous waist. His legs stuck out of his shorts like a pair of pink tree trunks. Not surprisingly, he was holding what looked like a forty-ounce clear cup that contained what was probably an orange smoothie. In most people's hands, the drink would have appeared cartoonish. In Rhett McCann's oversized paws, it was remarkably proportional.

"Rhett?" I said as I approached and stuck out my hand. "I'm Burnside."

He stood up ever-so-slightly, and grasped my hand. Shaking hands with Rhett McCann was like shaking hands with a catcher's mitt.

"Nice to meet you," he said. "Any friend of the X-man has to be good people."

"I've known Xavier for a few years. He's a good guy. Heckuva football player."

"Oh yeah. I played with him for a couple of years when I was with the Bills. Not much to do in Buffalo, we lived in the same condo complex. Played a lot of 2K and Smash with him. X's place was kind of a man cave."

"You from that part of the country?" I asked, taking a seat across from him.

"No. I'm a Texas boy. Played at U.T. Hoped to get drafted by the Cowboys, but you go where they want you to go. Buffalo for a while, now the Rams. Next year, who knows."

"You like it here?"

He reflected on this as he took a long sip of smoothie out of a straw that looked more like a golden tube of pasta. Plastic straws were being phased out in California, and restaurants were scrambling to find replacements.

"The weather's good and the Rams are doing well," he finally said. "We have a shot at the Super Bowl. But the people in this town? Look, I'm a down-home guy. Grew up in a small town. Like that kind of life."

"Understood," I said. "L.A.'s not for everyone."

"X told me that you were some kind of detective. Said you thought I could help you with a case."

"Yeah," I said and handed him my card. "Private investigator. Doing some background work on a girl you may know. Amanda Zeal."

Rhett snorted and put his drink down. "Yeah, I know her. Wish I didn't."

"What happened?"

"I had met her a few years ago. We came out here to play USC at the Coliseum."

I smiled. "We won that game."

"You're an SC guy?" he asked, eyeballing me carefully.

"Bleed cardinal and gold. Plus, I used to coach there. I think you played SC right after I left."

"Well, we gave you a beat down the next year in Austin,"

he countered. "Anyways, Amanda was working that one, interviewing guys before the game. I struck up a conversation when she was away from the cameras. Hot girl and all. Didn't think much of it, but when I moved here, X gave me her number. Said she was a lot of fun if you didn't mind the occasional drama."

"Okay."

"I didn't know anyone here, so I was looking to meet some people. Amanda was a partier, and we hit it off right away. But one thing I didn't know was that X had gone out with her in the off-season. Not that it mattered really. But I got the feeling he was trying to get away from her."

"Why would he do that?"

"I don't know. She's hot, but also a hot mess. Lots of fun at first. Always knew the right club or where the best party was. She knew her way around this town. We went out for a little while. But honestly, I wondered why she seemed so into me. Girl who looks like that, she could be with anyone. Not hard to tell, but I'm an oversized guy. Girls don't go out with me for my looks."

"Some girls like that," I said, trying to make sense of this. "Big guy like you. Maybe it makes them feel safe."

Rhett McCann shook his head. "She wasn't interested in safe. She was interested in money."

I frowned. I just wasn't getting why Amanda Zeal would be so interested in money. Wealthy parents, Beverly Hills upbringing, great job as an on-air reporter for Fox. Amanda was only twenty-four, and at that age, money was rarely front and center in importance. Not the way it becomes when a person reaches middle age, and has a family to take care of and a mortgage to pay.

"How much do you know about Amanda's background?" I asked.

He shrugged. "She went to Stanford, I heard she grew up rich. But that doesn't mean her parents handed her a trust fund. I got the feeling her parents weren't helping her at all. Not that they needed to. She was making good money with the network."

"Sounds a little puzzling," I said, resisting the impulse to scratch my head. "Tell me more about her."

"Okay. But what's your interest here? What did she do?"

I wondered about how best to respond to that without saying too much. "We're not really sure," I told him. "I'm honestly not certain where this investigation is going to lead. The more we know, the better. Maybe if you could tell me a little about what you guys did together, where you went with her, if you got introduced to any of her friends, that would help."

He thought for a minute. "We went to clubs. We talked about music, sports. She was big into football, I guess her dad was a football player in high school. Never played in college, it sounded like he might have regretted not doing so. She and I would talk about the games, I would explain stuff about how we broke down film. She was into it. Kind of cool. Not many girls are that interested."

"True," I said, thinking back to when I met Gail. She didn't know the difference between a quarterback and a first down, and no one in her family was a sports fan. It didn't matter to me, we found plenty of other things to talk about.

"She asked a lot of questions about teams. It was part of

her job to know about football, her being a sideline reporter and all."

I remembered something Grady Pinn had mentioned. "Did you notice Amanda ever get into it with coaches she interviewed during halftime?"

Rhett laughed. "Did I ever. Man, she had spunk. A girl getting into a head coach's face and demanding answers about his strategy? But she was, like, fearless."

"Did that strike you as a little strange?"

He pondered that. "Yeah. It kind of fits with her. She could be a drama queen at times. That became part of the problem I had with her. She was fun and hot and all. But she could be pushy and didn't like taking no for an answer."

"That's sometimes how a person gets ahead," I pointed out, not entirely sure I liked that, but I recognized it was more true than not.

"I guess. But she didn't know how to turn that part of her off when she wasn't in front of the camera."

"Oh yeah?"

"She was intense. Always after things. Wanted to know about the Rams, our offense, our defense, who's hurt, who's having personal issues. After a while, I started thinking it was a little weird, her doing college football."

"Maybe she was trying to move up to doing NFL games," I said.

"Wouldn't surprise me. She's competitive. I guess she was a swimmer in high school, she said she almost made the Olympic team, but got an injury during the trials. She's ambitious. Too ambitious, maybe, you know?"

I thought about ambition and I immediately thought

about Gail. When I met with Councilman Arthur Woo last month, he pointed that out about Gail. That she was ambitious, too. I didn't want to hold Gail back. When I wanted to go into coaching, she encouraged me to try something new, if I had that itch. Sometimes you just have to let things play out in life.

"You said something a minute ago. That she was really interested in money. Did she talk about that?" I asked.

"Nothing specific. I didn't think she had money problems at first. And I have a sixth sense when it comes to people trying to take advantage of me. Maybe it comes with growing up without a lot. Small town Texas and all. What we got, we worked for. And we don't just hand it to people for no good reason."

"How did she react to that?"

"Not well."

"She got mad?"

McCann hesitated and then looked down. "Worse than that. She stole ten thousand dollars from me."

My jaw dropped. "How did she manage that?"

"Got my password. Looking over my shoulder when I was online with my bank. Went in and transferred the money into her account the next day, some fake company. By the time I noticed it, she had closed down the account and the money was withdrawn. Gone."

"You're sure it was her?" I asked.

"It was her," he said definitively. "The money got transferred to a company called Breast Stroke LLC. Real cute, huh? It was her all right."

"You file a police report?"

"No."

I stared at him. "Why not?"

"Look, man. I'm not just a public figure. I'm a jumbo-size guy. If this got out, which it would if I filed a police report on a girl, I'd be a laughing stock. I'd never hear the end of it. I couldn't take that humiliation."

I stared at him some more. "For ten thousand dollars, I'd swallow a little pride and try and get my money back. Or have her put in jail. People aren't going to look down on you because you got robbed. It happens. It wasn't your fault. Plus, your background. You just said you don't like giving up money unless there's a good reason."

There was a moment of hesitation. "It wasn't just stealing," he finally said.

"Oh?"

"There was ... physical abuse. I can't let that get out."

Suddenly, things began to make some sense. The NFL no longer tolerated football players assaulting women, and it took pains to make examples of certain guys. Careers have ended over a single incident, and the lost earnings could pile up well into the millions.

"So you hit her," I said.

"You don't understand, Mr. Burnside."

"What's that?"

"I didn't hit her," he said, looking down. "She hit me."

Seven

Rhett McCann finally said he needed to get to practice, and I recognized I needed to eat lunch. The problem with eating lunch in an area you are only vaguely familiar with is that you default to those few restaurants with which you are vaguely familiar. In Calabasas, like much of the west Valley, the added problem was that the places I once frequented were now shuttered, or at best, in need of shuttering. The Valley was unfamiliar terrain to me, and the desire to try someplace new felt like it was more trouble than it was worth. There are days you just want to be surrounded by the familiar, whether or not it lives up to your hazy recollections.

I found my way to Sagebrush Cantina, known more to me for its countless beers on tap and endless opportunities for Saturday night hookups than for anything related to fine dining. But it did have the additional advantage of being close to the 101 freeway entrance, and that provided it with an extra-special status. I had last experienced Sagebrush Cantina more than a decade ago, the warm summer memories soaked with alcohol and pulsating with loud music. But on a late Thursday morning in January, it only offered a lifeless plate of enchiladas rancheros, forgettable beans and rice, and an incomprehensible lukewarm iced tea. The three occupied tables on the outdoor patio were filled with a group of soccer moms quaffing margaritas, a pair of aging bikers wearing denim vests over black t-shirts, laughing loudly and downing beers, and a suburban couple in their 60s, who were testing the waitress's patience by asking detailed questions about black beans and *frijoles refritos*. The place was sad in a way that a lot of vague memories were sad. When you try to relive them, they fail to stand the test of time, and this one failed miserably.

As I picked at my lunch, I tried to put the puzzle pieces in place on Amanda Zeal, but still, nothing quite snapped together. Her grandfather had all the telltale signs of a good cop gone bad. Her father was a successful businessman who was clever in the way deceitful men are clever, seizing an advantage and then getting his comeuppance. The men who had traversed through Amanda's love life did not have the best things to say about her. Her colleagues did not respect her. She came from wealth, earned a good living, and had a to-die-for job appearing on TV each week, mingling with famous coaches and athletes. Yet she was somehow in need of money, to the extent she might have stolen some. She had been involved in a couple of physical altercations. Her bodyguard and sometimes-boyfriend had been shot dead, and she had improbably disappeared. No one seemed to know where she was. I took a final spoonful of mediocre Spanish rice, threw some money on the table and walked out to my Pathfinder.

The drive back to the Westside was easy. Maybe the wide open freeways caused an innate relaxation, or maybe it was just idle curiosity that led me to call Drew Slick. But either way, the Beverly Hills Police Department seemed a logical next stop. I really had no next step, so this would be as good as it gets. The person answering the phone told me Detective Slick was in the office but not available to take calls. I took that to mean he was most likely eating lunch, and I also took that as an open invitation to swing by. I had nothing else planned for today, and even if the detective was not available, I could at least spend some time admiring what an idyllic City Hall should look like, that is, if a community had near-unlimited resources and a strong desire to impress. The Beverly Hills City Hall was an architectural masterpiece, replete with a soaring tower, a green mosaic-tile dome, and a gilded cupola crowning the top. It was a City Hall unlike any other, but if this type of ostentatious display belonged anywhere, it certainly belonged in Beverly Hills.

Unfortunately for the Beverly Hills PD, they were not housed within the confines of this spectacular City Hall, but rather, in a more pedestrian building on Rexford Drive, a block above little Santa Monica. The entrance doors were framed with a checkerboard design of light and dark blues, a curious pattern which might have been stylish in a different decade. It now came off as rather tired and worn, a curious piece of art which paled badly in comparison to the rest of the civic center. The police department was apparently unconcerned about properly impressing its guests.

Detective Slick had a phone cradled between his neck and

shoulder, his feet edged against a maple veneer desk, knees bent. His gun was on vivid display, tucked into a holster under his armpit. I knew enough to stow my weapons in the car before entering the premises. If there was one thing all police departments had in common, it was that they frowned upon an uninvited visitor entering their place of business packing a loaded handgun.

I waved to Detective Slick, and he looked at me for a long moment before turning his head away. I decided that was the closest I would get to a warm reception. I pulled over a metal folding chair and tried to make myself comfortable as I waited patiently for him to finish his call. I took out my phone and read an article about the upcoming Rams game. They were still favored to win.

"Oh, good, the private sector has arrived," Slick said, as he tossed his phone absently onto the desk. A half-full bottle of purple Vitamin Water sat nearby. "What do you have for me?"

"Funny, I was going to ask you the same thing," I said.

Slick sighed. "Here we go. Just when I was hoping you wouldn't be like all those other P.I.s."

"Sorry to disappoint. You crack the case yet?"

"Getting there," he responded with a wink.

"Oh... ?" I said, leaving the question hanging in the air, thus begging an answer. With cops there was no earthly guarantee they would ever bite, but Slick seemed to be in a good mood.

"Yeah," he started. "We're looking hard at the boyfriend, that Wyatt Angstrom. No alibi, no one can corroborate where he was after you left him. Said he was working in his office with the door closed, but that sounded fishy. He came off as nervous and so did that pea-brain assistant of his. Nothing Angstrom said adds up."

I nodded. "You search his home?"

"Sure. We kicked the door down and tossed the place. C'mon, Burnside. We're not going rogue here. But I have a funny feeling someone may be swearing out a search warrant any moment now. We take a dim view of homicide in Beverly Hills. This isn't the LAPD."

I thought about this and decided to keep the conversation professional. "He own a gun?"

"He does, but hey, so does half of California. Means nothing. We're still waiting on the autopsy results for Machado. Once we get a read on what kind of gun was used, that'll help. A little. But it's not evidence."

"You think the motive was jealousy?"

"You got something else?" he countered.

"Not really. But I still can't get that white van out of my head. The one from Star Rentals."

"Oh yeah, about that. We talked to their corporate office, they gave us a list of vehicles rented in the area in the past week. Ran the plates against our reader, we learned the van that entered city limits. Rented to some kid in Compton. My guys went out there last night and talked to him. Seemed nervous but we're good at making people nervous."

"Nothing there?"

"Nope. Kid's a mover. Said he rented the van to move someone who lived down the street from Amanda. Said a neighbor saw him working and had him come back the next day to move some furniture into storage. Had all the moving equipment, hand trucks, dollies. It added up."

"Lives in Compton?" I asked. "Not exactly around the corner."

Slick picked up the Vitamin Water and took a long swallow. "Westside real estate," he said, coming up for air and exhaling a loud breath of enjoyment. "Apartments are pricey around here. Got to make some coin to afford this area. No big surprise he lives somewhere else."

"You say he was nervous?"

Slick peered at me. "What? You really think there's something else there?"

"Maybe. It just doesn't fit well."

"You're over-thinking this."

"You mind if I talk to him?"

Drew Slick leaned back and thought. I sat and waited. Police detectives normally didn't like P.I.s snooping around their territory. But Slick was considering it. Maybe it was because this was Compton and not Beverly Hills, maybe it was because he had dismissed this mover as a suspect, or maybe it was because I was a former LAPD officer and not someone who got his PI license because he didn't like working as an insurance adjuster. But in the end, I think he became forthcoming because I gave him some good leads that were actually panning out. Tit for tat.

"I'll let you have a call with him. Name's Alex Solis. I think he lives on Orchard Street in Compton," he said, and he wrote a phone number down on a slip of paper. "Crappy neighborhood, but hey, it's Compton."

"Thanks," I said.

"You find out anything, I'm your first call. Got it?"

"Sure. By the way, anything come from that Mike White guy? The bookie Moose owed twenty large to?"

"Yeah, about that Mike White guy," he said, looking at the ceiling, "We haven't found him. There's about fifty Mike Whites in the region. We don't have the manpower to chase every lead down. Might not be his real name. And even if it were, he might not even live around here."

I looked around the office. It was pretty quiet, especially for a police station. I reminded myself this was Beverly Hills. I also debated whether I should detail my morning conversations with a pair of NFL football players who had had a skittish relationship with Amanda Zeal. But Amanda's name hadn't been mentioned yet. I wondered if Slick and his team had even bothered to check into her whereabouts. I wondered if there was a Starbucks nearby. I turned back to him.

"So, any luck in finding Amanda?" I asked.

Slick gave a shrug of the shoulders. "She's in the wind. Hasn't come back to her apartment, we confirmed with her parents. They haven't seen her, haven't been able to make contact. Might be in her boyfriend's apartment, but like I said we're not kicking any doors in yet. I take it you haven't come across her."

"No," I said. "I've talked to a couple of guys who knew her. Seems like she may have money problems."

Slick's eyebrows raised. "Money problems, you say. That's plenty interesting. Something her and Machado had in common."

"Yeah, maybe that was all they had in common. But Amanda grew up in Beverly Hills, her parents are loaded, and she has a job that pays her a bundle. None of this quite makes sense."

"Oh, I don't know. I've worked this beat for fifteen years. Some people with big houses also have some pretty big debts. Not everything's the way it seems around here."

To that I agreed. And I knew that when it came to money, enough was never enough for some people. Maybe that was the case with Amanda. I had occasionally come across people whose sole goal in life was to collect a pile of money and to see that pile grow and grow, even if they had to steal it. Some people accumulated enough money to secure the next three generations in their line, but they still kept pushing for more. After a while, it stopped being about making enough to live well, it evolved into a game, a pursuit, practically an addiction. They would beg, borrow, or steal money in the hopes of leveraging it to get more. And sometimes people forgot that there were consequences to every action. Mismanaging money with the wrong people could be lethal, and you often didn't get many warnings. I had a funny feeling Moose Machado would have agreed.

*

I found a Starbucks three blocks from the Beverly Hills PD headquarters, parked, and brought in my iPad. There were about a dozen layabouts in there, all by themselves, all huddled over their various devices. I suspect some were unemployed, some were aspiring screenwriters, some were possibly both. I ordered a cup of *Guatamala Antigua* and waited a few minutes for a young woman to pack up her laptop and get up from a tall barstool. Two seconds after she slid off, I climbed on.

Calling Alex Solis posed a problem, because if he were involved in any criminal activity, it was unlikely he'd stay on the line for long. I decided I needed a personal visit. The only problem was that I didn't have his exact address.

There were five people named Alex Solis living in Compton, but none were under the age of forty, and none of them lived on Orchard Street. There was a strong possibility he might well be living with family, and if so, he'd be flying under the radar. I tried a reverse phone lookup, but that yielded nothing. Finally, I decided to get creative and call the number Drew Slick gave me. He picked up on the first ring.

"Yo, it's Ax."

"Hello. I'm calling for Alex Solis," I said in my most bureaucratic voice.

"Yeah. Who's this?" he demanded.

"This is the phone company. We have some unusual charges on your bill. Did you make any international calls today, sir?"

"Did I what?"

I looked at the phone for a minute and then repeated myself.

"No. Why? Someone using my number?"

"It appears as if that's the case. Look, if you didn't make the calls, we can take off the charges."

"You damn well better. I ain't paying for no one else's calls."

"We're happy to do that, but I just need a little information. Your name is Alex Solis and you live in

Compton, California?"

"Damn right I do."

"Please verify your mailing address."

"My what?"

"Your mailing address," I repeated. "That way we can send you a statement telling you that you don't have to pay for these charges."

"Oh, yeah. I'm at 1891 Orchard. You get that thing off my bill, you hear?"

"Yes, sir," I smiled. "We'll do that posthaste."

"Say what?"

"Right away."

The line went dead, but the smile remained on my face, at least until I checked traffic. There were a lot of long red lines on the southbound Largo Beach freeway out of downtown and headed in the direction of Compton. I gave it a long look and then decided my meeting with Alex Solis could wait a day.

I called the Largo Beach Police Department and left a message for Bart Sokolov. Then I scanned through the internet, first checking the football news and then moving on to politics. Shane Karp's announcement that he was running for City Attorney did not merit a mention on the home page of the *L.A. Times* website, but I did see a puff piece on Arthur Woo. The story detailed Arthur's Ivy League education at Columbia and his numerous accomplishments as an L.A. City Councilman. He deflected questions about his possible run for mayor, and while he heaped praise upon the candidates already in the race, he did not call out any by name. It was mentioned in the article, though, that a leading candidate for mayor was Jay Sutker, the current City Attorney.

I pulled myself away from the news about sports and politics, and began scouring the web for anything related to a certain Gail Pepper. I spent a good thirty minutes rifling through news, social media, and a variety of search engines. All I learned was that my wife, sparkling as she was in person, had a remarkably dull online presence. She grew up in Costa Mesa, her father was a high school history teacher, she graduated from UCLA *summa cum laude*, was a member of Kappa Alpha Theta, and played intramural soccer. She earned a law degree from Berkeley, and had made donations to the Downtown Women's Shelter. She had no Facebook profile, no Twitter feed, and there was nothing on Instagram. I found a few photos from high school that her friends had posted online, and as pretty as she was as a teenager, the photos were more endearing than risqué. The most outlandish thing I could find on Gail was that in college she won a sorority contest for being the girl who ate the most spicy chicken wings in a five minute period. If there was anything unsavory she had done in her life, a political operative was unlikely to discover it. In fact, the most subversive and dangerous act she ever engaged in was most likely marrying me.

I moved on to Gail's colleague and possible rival, Shane Karp, and things got a little more salacious. Shane Karp had a lively online persona, mostly posting tame photos on Facebook and judicious tweets on Twitter. A simple Google search only turned up some criminal cases he had worked on as a prosecutor. But it's often the third and fourth pages of

Google search results that lead you to some interesting clues. I jotted down the high school Shane attended in northern California, and the names of his friends and acquaintances. While Shane's Facebook page had likely been scrubbed clean, one of his friends, Larry Beets, treated Facebook very differently. Photos of alcohol-laced parties and half-naked embraces were common, and Larry was kind enough to have made all six hundred of the lurid photos he uploaded available for anyone to view. Either he didn't know about the privacy switch or he didn't care.

By the time I got to the two-hundredth photo, I hit pay dirt. There were photos of Larry and Shane hugging various girls, their hands plastered over a multitude of private parts, as well as images of them chugging liquor straight out of the bottle. The two looked like they were barely out of their teens, but the caption made it very clear that Larry and Shane were celebrating. A lot. The topper was a photo of a pair of shot glasses filled with amber liquid sitting precariously atop the bare breasts of a nubile, smiling, and most likely inebriated young woman, with the two young men next to her, each with their tongue against a breast to balance a shot glass. There was ostensibly nothing illegal about what they were doing. But these images were clearly not emblematic of a future civic leader.

I took a screen shot of the photo and sat back. How best to approach Gail with this sort of tawdry bit of excess was not the easiest thing to figure out. To say Gail had better morals and ethics than I did was like saying the sun rose in the east. She prosecuted criminals but always did it by the book. I, on the other hand, investigated a variety of shady characters and made up the rules as I went. Gail and I were an odd match, but ostensibly a logical one. Opposites attract. Yin and yang. She would take the moral high ground, I would stake out the more practical space, which sometimes wound up being in a sewer. But Gail was now entering a world where people's characters were maligned for sport, and where living a decent life was irrelevant. If you ran for public office you also ran the risk of going up against an unethical rival who would do anything to win. Twisting the truth, misrepresenting facts, or even just making up outrageous claims were an accepted part of politics today. I concluded Gail would never use a photo like this as a means of attack, a method for winning an election. But I also knew she needed to have something in the chamber, just in case. In the event Shane Karp went into gutter mode, she might need to follow suit. Or have someone do it for her. I recognized I had severe limitations in knowing how to work as a political operative. Fortunately, I knew someone who was well-versed in the not-so-subtle art of bare-knuckled political campaigning.

Arthur Woo's assistant put me on hold for a few minutes before coming back on the line and telling me the erstwhile city councilman could see me at four o'clock today. I shivered as I imagined what the traffic would be like, but I had ninety minutes to get to Koreatown. Even though the 10 freeway was jammed, there was always surface streets. I packed my iPad and grabbed the rest of my coffee. The things you do for love.

I arrived at Arthur's district office on Vermont Avenue, just north of Wilshire. He worked out of a nondescript office befitting a public servant, but it was full of noise and movement, staffers walking up and down the hallways with a sense of urgency and a sense of purpose. Some were having conversations on phones as they walked, others simply moved along quickly. All seemed to be carrying iPads, file folders, or sheets of paper in their hands. All were Korean.

A thin, pretty young woman with black-framed glasses led me into Arthur's office. She asked if I would like some tea. I politely declined. She left, closing the door behind her, and I waited for Arthur Woo to stop his intense concentration on a document in front of him and acknowledge my presence. He did, albeit after a good ten seconds.

"Mr. Burnside," he said, finally standing and shaking my hand. "It's good to see you again. And so soon."

"The pleasure's all mine, Councilman. Thank you for taking time out of your schedule."

"Have you reconsidered my proposal to head up our security detail? A mayor of this city needs good people around him. You'd be doing your civic duty."

I smiled as we both sat down. "I'm sorry, Arthur. That's not in my immediate plans."

"A shame'" he said. "I'll have to find another way of securing your vote in June. That is, if you're a Democrat."

"I'll vote for you," I told him. "And I'm thinking of turning in my independent credentials and signing up for your party."

"Wonderful. You've seen the light, Mr. Burnside. I'm so happy," he replied, without smiling or doing anything that seemed remotely close to being happy.

"I've seen no such light, Arthur. And frankly I don't have a lot of use for either party. But I'll vote for you whenever you're running."

This time I saw the slightest movement between Arthur Woo's lips, the slightest crack, the smallest glint of what might have been the start of a smile or simply a trace of intrigue. "This can't be because of my policy positions," he observed.

"It's not."

"I know. I don't have any."

I felt my eyebrows raising. "You don't?"

"Not yet. They'll be released in due time. My plans for remaking Los Angeles into the world-class city it should be. I have big plans. They'll come out soon enough. No sense rushing things. Elections are a process. You have to let them unfold."

"I'll remember that," I said.

"But you have triggered my curiosity, Mr. Burnside. Pleasantly, of course. Why would you vote for me without knowing my positions on the issues?"

"I'll vote for you because you're smart, and I don't think you'd ever do anything that wasn't smart. I don't know how you'd transform L.A. if you were mayor, but I doubt you'd do anything to make it worse. But the main reason I'd vote for you is simply that I know you. And you'll take my calls and you'll meet with me. I don't pretend to understand much about politics, but I do know that having access to important people at the right moment can sometimes be a turning point in someone's life. That life might be mine."

Arthur nodded appreciatively. "Of all the reasons for voting for someone, that's not one I hear often. But it's one that makes a world of sense. And one day I might need a favor from you, too. We're all human. And we do have a tendency to take care of those who take care of us. Friendship is a valued commodity."

I never really considered Arthur Woo a friend, but in his world, friendship often came with some unique criteria. Friendships in politics were more like relationships, bonding over certain issues, separating over others. There were worse people to have as friends than rising political stars. And the reality was that I liked interacting with smart people. Metal sharpens metal.

"So what brings you down to our lovely neighborhood today, Mr. Burnside?"

"I need a lesson in politics."

This time Arthur Woo actually did give a tiny smile. "Well, I suppose you came to the right place. Tell me more."

"I'm sure you know that the City Attorney announced his run for mayor."

"Ah, yes. The esteemed, Mr. Sutker. Yes, I did see his announcement."

"And by running for mayor, Sutker won't be running for re-election as City Attorney. So there'll be a spirited campaign for the City Attorney's office this year."

"There will."

"My wife Gail is thinking of throwing her hat in the ring. You were right about her, Arthur. She has a level of ambition. You also said you thought she'd be good at it."

"I did indeed. And I'm pleased to hear she's considering it. I hope you'll encourage her."

"I've told her I'll support her in whatever she does. But politics is foreign to me. And I know what it's like to be in the public eye and for all the wrong reasons. I don't want her to get caught up in what I was caught up in."

Arthur's expression grew serious. "Your background. That teenage girl."

"Yes," I said, not surprised Arthur knew about me. Arthur Woo's knowledge ran far and wide and deep. My tenure as an LAPD officer ended unceremoniously, unsubstantiated charges leading me to resign from the police force. I had never committed any of the felonies I was accused of committing, but my name would always be linked with them. And in the end, it was my own rogue behavior that led me down the path toward being terminated. I could accept the public scrutiny that came with my downfall; I did not want Gail to bear that burden, too.

"The public has a way of discounting things over time, Mr. Burnside. This circumstance that happened to you ten years ago will come up again at some point. Maybe a political rival will float it, maybe a journalist will resurrect it. Gail will need to have a ready answer, and you'll need to make a public statement. But I can assure you, the media is fickle. The news cycle is constant. There will always be another story to push that off the front page. In L.A. it could be as simple as a rainstorm. And people will forget about it and move on. The public can be very fickle, too. But they are forgiving. Los Angeles is a city of second chances. I'm sure you know that."

"All right," I said. "That makes sense. But I have another issue I'd appreciate your advice on. If my wife enters the race for City Attorney she will be up against Shane Karp. I've uncovered some unsavory information about Mr. Karp's background. I know my wife won't approve of using it against him in a campaign."

"But you wish to do so anyway."

I rubbed my chin. "The thought crossed my mind."

"Mr. Burnside, that may not be necessary. And if I may guide you to a better path, I believe your wife should disassociate herself from Mr. Sutker. The current City Attorney is not someone she should, how can I put this delicately, get into bed with. In a metaphorical way, of course."

"Of course," I started. "And you'd like Gail to endorse you for mayor over Jay Sutker."

"That would be wonderful, but I'm only offering advice at this stage. Certainly, I'd love to have your beautiful wife endorse me and campaign with me. I'm building a team that includes a slate of councilmen, the county assessor and a member of the board of supervisors. Including the next City Attorney would be helpful to both of us. But that's not what I was about to suggest."

"Just what, then, were you about to suggest?"

"Mr. Sutker is going to run into some problems in his campaign. Certain information will be released in good time, and if all goes as planned, he will most likely drop out of the campaign and resign from his position as City Attorney. I can't go into too many details, other than he has made some very bad judgments. He is going to be disgraced, and your wife should capitalize on this opportunity."

I stared at him as I let this sink in. I was learning a valuable lesson that my political science professor at USC never bothered to touch upon. "Please tell me more. How might she ... capitalize on this turn of events?"

"First, she needs to have Mr. Sutker endorse her opponent, Shane Karp. The way to do that is for her to attack something Mr. Sutker has done as City Attorney. It doesn't matter what. What matters is that she gets under his skin just enough to push him to endorse her opponent. Do you see where this is going?"

I nodded. "Because by enabling Mr. Sutker to embrace her opponent in the primary, Shane Karp will get caught up in the same net that brings down Jay Sutker. And Gail will be able claim the moral high ground."

"You're learning fast, Mr. Burnside."

"We just have to trust you, Arthur."

"Admittedly, that is true. And I understand why that might give you pause. My being the brother of Justin Woo. I do recall you worked for his opponent, the former governor. The venerable Rex Palmer."

I smiled a little. "Rex was a client. I can't say I was his biggest supporter."

"I take it you voted for Mr. Palmer."

"Would it surprise you if I told you I honestly can't remember?" I said.

"You're an interesting man, Mr. Burnside. And I think you're seeing how to play your cards well."

"So let me ask you a direct question, Arthur. You're a very bright man. And an expert in politics. Be realistic. What type of a chance does Gail have to get elected?"

Arthur gave me a long look. "Others are bound to jump in the race. She'll need money. If she can raise enough, she'll be competitive."

"I have an idea on how to work on the fundraising," I said,

the idea literally just popping into my head at that very moment. "You reminded me of something. But again, what would you say her chances are?"

Arthur continued to give me a long look as he contemplated his next remark. "You're familiar with the sport of boxing, aren't you, Mr. Burnside?"

"Quite."

"I'd say, on the whole, the best assessment I can give you is that she has a puncher's chance."

I bit my lower lip at his comment, and took a breath. "That bad?" I asked.

"No, Mr. Burnside," he replied and offered a wide smile. "That good."

Eight

On the slog home from Koreatown, I called Gail and took her through my idea. She was hesitant but intrigued. In the end, she agreed, most likely recognizing that as the campaign started becoming real, the ramifications of what was involved were setting in. After we hung up, I switched to a burner phone, placed a call, and hung up when a woman answered. That was what I needed to know.

Traffic finally busted loose after Robertson. I picked up Gail and we dropped Marcus with the Hartnetts for an extended play date. Sailing into Santa Monica, I navigated north on Ocean Avenue, marveling at the dark purple-blue ocean lined against the golden setting sun. When southern California has a pretty day, it is like a strutting peacock, preening and effortlessly showing off its inherent beauty. I turned right onto Adelaide and found parking up the street from our destination, not far from the Santa Monica Stairs. It had been years since I last visited this breathtaking home, and I drank in the luxury as we strolled along the wide front lawn. Everything was going smoothly until I knocked on the door. A man answered, and after glancing briefly at Gail, he stared at me like I was a visitor from another planet.

"Hello, Governor," I said, framing a phony smile on my face.

"Former Governor. But, yes. Hello there."

"I hope you've been well."

He looked at me warily, and didn't bother to answer my question. "Are you here on ... business?"

"In a way. May I come in?"

Former Governor Rex Palmer gave this topic a too-long moment of consideration before I heard Crystal Fairborn's voice call out to ask who was at the door. I half-expected Rex to say "no one" and slam the door in my face, but I suspect he knew the futility of going forward with an exercise like that. I'd simply keep knocking.

"It's a special, surprise visitor," he said, opening the door and motioning us inside. "One who needs no introduction. At least he brought along his better half."

I walked into the spacious living room of a historic craftsman home, an early twentieth century marvel, redesigned for twenty-first century conveniences. There was a skylight, two working fireplaces, and high-beamed ceilings. Three Persian rugs lined the floor. Elaborate furniture was in full view, no doubt selected with the help of an expensive designer who took great pains to make the interior look as if it were laid out effortlessly. Crystal Fairborn had been sitting on an overstuffed sofa reading a book, but when she saw me, she quickly rose.

"Oh my goodness," she said, moving forward to give me a

big hug. "Special surprise indeed!"

"Can I get you two a drink?" asked Rex.

"Water would be fine," I said. "Maybe add some crushed ice, Governor?"

Rex Palmer looked at Gail who shook her head no. Or maybe she was just shaking her head. The governor chuckled and walked off, returning a minute later, handing me a glass of cold water that had no ice in it. I took the glass, gave it a sip, offered Rex an approving nod, and eased down onto a taupe love seat. Gail slipped in next to me, as Rex and Crystal sat on the sofa directly across from us.

"How is everything with the newlyweds?" I asked.

"I don't know if we still qualify as newlyweds," Crystal laughed. "But things are great. And we have you to thank for it."

"In an odd way," Rex added.

Odd indeed. Years ago, Rex Palmer had hired me to find his wayward teenage daughter while he was in the midst of a nasty re-election campaign against Arthur's brother, Justin Woo. I didn't so much find his daughter as she paraded into my office after a few days of searching; she had been holed up in her grandfather's Brentwood estate. She arrived with a ten thousand dollar check and her grandfather's instructions to keep her out of sight until the campaign was over. I squirreled her away temporarily at Crystal's house, as I found myself entangled in more intra-family issues than I really wanted. Seeing me probably brought back a wave of emotions for the governor; my guess was there had to be more bad than good. Rex lost that election in a veritable landslide, but he did find the love of his life in Crystal

Fairborn. So in an unusual way, I got to play Cupid, although that was the last thing I expected, and the last thing I intended. Sometimes the world rearranges things for the good.

"And how is your daughter?" I asked. "Molly, I believe her name was."

"She's in college. Back east. NYU. Majoring in spending money."

I smiled. "Kids today. At least you can afford it."

"My family has been very generous to us," he acknowledged.

"Your dad still around?" I asked. Burnside, the great conversationalist.

"Pushing eighty, but still here. Plays golf three times a week and complains about the Democrats the rest of the time."

We all smiled together. "He's charming in his own way," Crystal added.

"I guess you have a mixed marriage," I said. "Democrat and Republican."

"We try and minimize political discussions," Crystal said. "Keeps the home civil."

"Good idea," I remarked, taking an uneasy glance over at Gail. "What have you been doing, Governor? Have you left politics for good?"

Rex Palmer sighed. "I took a partnership in a law firm. I sit on the boards of a few companies. Crystal and I are starting the Wayne Foundation. A testament to her first husband. Deals with homeless issues."

I paused. The homeless population in L.A. was ever-growing. But Crystal's first husband, Wayne Fairborn, was an advocate of helping the homeless re-enter society as productive members. He was also an aspiring politician in his own right, a candidate for mayor in our nearby seaside town of Bay City, until someone shot him to death in his office.

"Nice way to memorialize him," I finally said. "Wayne would have approved."

"We like to think so," he said. "And in answer to the second part of your question, I have mostly retired from politics. I still get inquiries about being a delegate to the convention, and once in a while someone floats my name as head of the state Republican party. But I've deflected those. I like private life."

"Understood," I said uneasily. "But that brings me to why we're here."

"Politics?" Crystal asked, eyes growing a little wide.

I nodded. "Ours, not yours."

"I see," she said. "That's different. I'm not up for being a political spouse. Too many bad memories. I just couldn't go through that again."

"I get it," I said. Wayne's gruesome murder still affected me. Obviously, it would affect Crystal forever. That Wayne didn't die at the hands of a political assassin was not much comfort. And the idea that I was about to become a political spouse brought the morbid topic of mortality front and center, very suddenly and very harshly. I had not thought of Wayne in a while, and I had clearly not thought about everything else surrounding Gail's possible entrée into a very public life. I had not fully steeled myself for the possible realities, ones that could be severe and unforgiving and in a few instances, tragic. Seeing Rex, and especially seeing Crystal, put those in the forefront of my mind.

"So what exactly is going on?" she asked.

"Gail here is thinking of running for City Attorney. She's an ACA in that office now. Jay Sutker's running for mayor, which means there will be a vacancy."

Rex stood up. "Sweetheart, I'll let you discuss this in private. I have some work to do," he said and turned to me. "It was nice seeing you again, Burnside."

"Same here," I said.

He smiled graciously at Gail as he walked out. I wasn't entirely sure how nice it was to see me again, especially since it was obvious to him that we were here to solicit money, lessening the family coffers by requesting a campaign contribution. I watched him walk out of the room and then I turned to Crystal.

"Has Rex ever gotten over the election loss?"

Crystal gazed across the room for a minute. "He doesn't talk about it. But I think there's still a wound there. It may always be there. Losing an election is hard. And it wasn't just losing, he was voted out of office, and by a wide margin. It might have been easier if he could rationalize it by saying it was the economy or something external. But he knows he made some big mistakes. At least he's trying to find other things in his life."

"I'm sure meeting you helped."

"I'm sure it did, too," she smiled. "And we do have you to thank for that. Even though you didn't plan on it."

"Often that's how the best things in life happen. I met Gail when I was investigating a case on campus."

"I wondered how you two met."

Gail spoke. "I was working as a security guard. Didn't quite know what I wanted to do with my life after college, and that seemed interesting. Law enforcement was more exciting than working in corporate life. But eventually I realized I wasn't meant to be just a security guard. It was a great experience for a couple of years, but I needed something more. That led to law school which led to becoming a prosecutor. And now maybe to something else."

"Which brings you here," Crystal observed.

"Are we that overt?"

Crystal smiled. "I'm used to it. We get approached a lot. Mostly by charities, but occasionally by candidates."

"How do you normally respond?" I asked.

"Most of the time we decline," she said. "As I mentioned, it helps to keep politics out of our marriage. But you're a special case."

I smiled. "I am indeed special."

She threw back her head and laughed. "Well, I take it you're looking for a donation."

Gail leaned forward. "My wonderful and creative husband hatched this idea. I'm a little reluctant, and probably more than a little awkward because I've never done this before. I apologize if I'm doing it badly. Are you open to discussing it?"

"You're not doing it at all badly. You're being sincere. If you were too smooth, I'd be concerned. And yes, we can certainly discuss it. I remember the two of you attended our wedding. I've met you, but only briefly. I assume you're a

Democrat?"

"She is," I piped in. "And she'd make a great City Attorney. I'm biased of course, but she is one of the smartest people I've ever met, and she also has an ethical streak that not many people have. She always seems to know the right thing to do. And If there's one thing I can guarantee you, she won't ever make you sorry if you back her campaign."

She nodded enthusiastically. "That's good to know. I'd like to help make the world a better place."

"I should also tell you why I want to run," Gail said. "I think the City Attorney's office has a world of possibility. But I don't feel it's being run as effectively as it could be. It's far too political. Decisions on who to prosecute and how to negotiate plea bargains should be done for the good of the community. As well as looking at the criminal being prosecuted. And there's also been too much grandstanding. I'd like to get the office back to where it should be."

"There have been some very high-profile trial losses," Crystal remarked. "What you're saying makes a lot of sense. But how long do you think you'd stay in this position?"

Gail licked her lips. "I'm not sure. Are you're asking if I would be coming back to you in a few years to request more support in running for a higher office?"

"That is indeed what I'm asking."

"My guess is no. I'm committed to the City Attorney's office. But I can't rule out what you've suggested. Not entirely anyway. The world changes, and sometimes you have to change with it. Duty calls."

"Indeed," Crystal said, looking at Gail and then at me. "I must tell you something."

"What's that?" I asked.

"You chose well."

I looked at Gail and caught her blushing for a brief instant. I felt like I might be blushing, too. "I did indeed. Very well. I was lucky to meet her and lucky to win her heart."

"Sometimes life leads you to a good place. Even if you have to go through some dark moments. It just takes time."

I agreed. For me it had taken a very long time. But I was glad I was where I was at. I thought of something and turned back to Crystal. "Would your making a campaign contribution pose any problem for Rex?"

She paused for a moment. "If he were still active in politics it might. He's obviously a Republican, albeit a moderate one, if that label actually exists any more. But politics are over for him. So I don't think it would be a problem. The money from Wayne's estate is, well, substantial. We're well off and we don't have kids. Rex's daughter will be well taken care of by her grandfather. My father is getting on in years, but he'll be fine."

"Speaking of which, how is Serge doing?"

"Still strong as a mule, and twice as stubborn," she said, and then added a wistful comment, "And my sister is out of the picture."

"Yes. Let me ask you something," I started, my curiosity getting the best of me. I probably shouldn't have inquired, but there are a lot of things I shouldn't be doing. "What do people do with their money when they don't have children to leave it to? Give it to charity?"

"Sure, some of it. There are people who want to leave a

legacy, which is how hospital wings get built, and how universities add new buildings. Other people just spend it down. That might be difficult in our case. We have too much of it."

"Nice problem to have," I smiled. "And I hope we haven't been too forward with our request. Neither of us are skilled at asking people for money. When I ask for favors, I at least try to have something to offer in return."

"You never know," she said with a wink. "I might call upon one of you to do me a favor someday."

I glanced over at Gail and she glanced back at me. We were getting an advanced education in the curious world of politics. The lessons seemed to be handed down by the minute.

*

My phone buzzed on the way home, and the detective from the Largo PD was on the other line. Bart Sokolov said he'd meet me tomorrow morning, that is, if I were inclined to drive down to Largo Beach for breakfast before he started work. He spoke glowingly of a beachside diner that served the kind of waffles worth driving out of your way for. I agreed to meet, but was quickly reminded I was dealing with a cop here. Their hours are not the hours of most people. But the drive to Largo Beach would, at least, be a breeze before the crack of dawn.

I slept fitfully, and could have used a few more hours, but that wasn't in the cards this morning. I sensed it was going to be a long day. The temperature was pleasant when I left Mar

Vista at five-fifteen, but it was also a bellwether that this afternoon would be on the warm side.

Polly's Pies was a chain coffee shop, and I used to frequent its Santa Monica restaurant until it abruptly closed one day, replaced by another chain coffee shop that wasn't nearly as good. In addition to clear traffic, the other nice part about an early morning rendezvous was I could find parking in front of the restaurant. Bart Sokolov was easy to find. Even though he sat in a round booth in the far corner of the restaurant, there just weren't many people eating breakfast yet. He was a thick man in his early fifties, wearing a blue windbreaker and sporting a walrus mustache. All he needed was a pile of doughnuts sitting next to him to scream cop. He was already digging into breakfast, not doughnuts, but a large plate of waffles with an overload of maple syrup dripping off the edges of the crust.

"Good morning," I said, slipping across from him in the booth.

"Burnside, huh?" he said, shoving a forkful of sticky looking waffles into his mouth and chewing vigorously.

"That's me. Thanks for agreeing to meet."

"Don't get too comfortable," he said, wiping his mouth with a paper napkin, swallowing, and rising from the table. "I got to take a leak. Follow me."

With that, he waddled across the restaurant with me in tow, and I wondered just what kind of a show he had in store for me at this hour. We entered the small men's room, and he opened the stalls one by one to make sure we were alone. Then he turned to face me.

"Okay, look. I'm sorry, but I got to do this. If you want to talk, that is."

I stared at him. "You want to frisk me?"

"Only way we talk. You can save me the trouble and tell me if you're wearing a wire."

"No wire," I told him. "But I have to tell you I'm packing. Got a .357 under my left armpit. My guess is that a wire's a bigger a concern for you."

"Got that straight. No, I checked you out. You're former LAPD. I'd be surprised if you weren't carrying anything. But still. Why don't you turn around. This won't take long. You know the drill."

I knew the drill for frisking someone for a weapon, but never for recording equipment. This was normally mob stuff. The only ones who were concerned about someone wearing a wire were people who were about to have a private conversation they didn't want anyone else to hear. That alone made going through the frisking acceptable, although Detective Sokolov was remarkably thorough in his procedure.

"Sorry about that, buddy," he said as we walked back to the table. "But it's part of the deal."

"I don't know if I should be ordering breakfast now or having a cigarette," I said as we slid back into the booth.

He laughed and picked up his fork. "Try the Belgian waffles. If you're tough enough to handle the whipped cream."

A waitress came over, and I ordered black coffee and plain waffles, butter and syrup on the side. Sokolov snorted and told me I sounded like an L.A. guy.

"That's not far from Culver City," I said, as the waitress

returned with a steaming cup of black coffee. I took a sip. It wasn't bad for a diner, but I'd need to drink twice as much to get the same jolt as I got from a Starbucks roast.

"Nope," he said. "I like living there. My kids went to school at Culver High, the education was decent. Plus, they both played football and liked playing for the coach. My eldest got into some trouble, but he worked through it with them. I guess you know Coach Fultz."

"I do. He was my coach, as well."

"Been there a long time, I guess."

"I think he started coaching when I got there," I said with a wink.

Sokolov snorted again and took another big bite of a waffle. "So what can I do you for?" he asked. "You said something about Ed Zellis."

"I did. You know him well?"

He nodded. "Well enough. I was getting going with the department around the time he was finishing up. We overlapped for a few years. But he was my training officer when I first went into plainclothes. Was supposed to teach me the ropes. I got quite a lesson, let me assure you."

"What can you tell me?"

"I could tell you plenty, but I won't. Not yet anyway. First tell me your interest."

"Like I mentioned on the phone. I've been a P.I. for about ten years now since I left the LAPD. I'm working a case regarding Ed's granddaughter. Name's Amanda Zeal. Her father hired me to find out about an assault that happened to her a few nights ago. He also hired a bodyguard who quickly ended up dead. Amanda disappeared, so my next task is to try and find her."

"Okay," he said, still chewing. "How does that involve Largo Beach?"

"I'm not sure that it does or doesn't. But I'm running out of leads. And no disrespect, but I'm aware of Largo Beach's reputation. I don't know that Amanda has a connection with this place or the police department, but I suspect her grandfather was a dirty cop. Let's just say I've found that where there's smoke, there's fire. Maybe there's nothing here, maybe there's something. I won't know until I ask."

Sokolov chewed and listened. I finally picked up the coffee and took another sip. He put his fork down and looked out the window at the black sky.

"I started off here like most cops start off. Driving a patrol car. Did that for years and then moved into plainclothes. I knew all about Largo being a port city, and port cities are often where the drugs come in. Seemed like an interesting gig. My first plainclothes assignment was in narcotics. And my first collar was with Ed and his partner, Jimbo Thomas. That was also the last collar I got in narcotics."

"Tell me about it."

"We did this sting, okay. Four of us, including Ed, Jimbo, and this sergeant, Kim Sponsler. We took the dogs onto some of the boats that came in from Colombia. Sniff out drugs. They found coffee grounds, so we knew we were onto something. Pried the crate open and saw three kilos of blow. Tagged it and waited for the guys to come pick 'er up. We followed them back to an apartment on Pine. Two guys were waiting for them, we let them go into the apartment and then, two minutes later, we kicked the door down. That was the fun part."

I frowned. "Coffee grounds. How could the sniffer dogs find it? Won't coffee throw them off the scent?"

"At one time it did. Smugglers used coffee grounds to hide the smell of the drugs. So we just started training the dogs to sniff through the coffee. Pretty simple. The dealers didn't catch on for a long time. Crooks aren't the brightest lights."

"True."

"Yeah, well, anyways, we nabbed these clowns with over a hundred grand worth of blow. Plus, we picked up thirty grand in cash. That's where things went off the rails."

"Because the cash disappeared," I said.

"Most of it. I didn't take the evidence, my job was to book the perps. When they were arraigned, they were charged with possession, but only half the blow went in as evidence and there was no mention of any money. The perps weren't about to say anything, so it all went unnoticed."

"You say anything?"

"I was thinking how I'd approach them. But then something funny happened. I was getting into my car one night to go home and noticed a package on the floor of the backseat. There was five grand in cash sitting there. No note, nothing written, just a wad of bills stuffed into a big envelope."

"What'd you do?"

"I was kind of jammed up, you know. I wasn't about to keep it, but I couldn't give it back. It was a blank envelope, who would I give it to? Offer it to Ed or Jimbo, and they'd just smirk and ask what I was talking about. I finally decided to transfer out of narcotics. A few days later, Ed comes up to me in the squad room and asks if I got a package recently. He had this mean little smile on him. I looked him dead in the eye and said I didn't know what he was talking about. No idea. He watched me pretty close for a while, but eventually he left me alone. He knew I wouldn't rat him out."

"It's called balance of terror," I told him, thinking back to my international politics class at SC.

Sokolov scrunched up his nose. "What's that?"

"It's where both parties have something to lose. I think it might have been a military term once. Imagine two countries where both have nuclear weapons. Neither one can use them on the other country, because if one did, the other would simply launch their own nuclear weapons in response. If one country deployed these weapons, it would assure their own destruction. Balance of terror means both sides are scared to utilize what they have."

At that point, the waitress came by with my plate of waffles. I tried a bite without butter or syrup and decided it was uninspiring. I picked up the small pitcher of maple syrup and poured a generous amount over the waffles, making sure to distribute it evenly.

"Interesting. Yeah, Ed wasn't going to run me out of the department, because he knew I had something on him. Better to let sleeping dogs lie."

"Pretty much," I said, taking a bite with syrup and liking it more. "So what did you do with the money?"

Sokolov paused and glanced around the restaurant. "I thought of giving it to charity. But it would have to be anonymous, I couldn't have anything traced back to me. That's tricky. But a friend of mine was having health issues back then, heart problems, he had a bad ticker. Needed to pay his medical bills. Let's just say a package wound up in his car."

"Charity begins at home," I observed.

"Well, I couldn't keep it and I couldn't give it back. Imagine trying to deal with that kind of dilemma. Tossing it off the Largo Pier was my only other option. I can live with how things ended up. I got caught in something and found a way out."

I agreed. The money was a double-edged sword, a blessing and a curse. If he had gone and flashed it around like some small-time hood who suddenly got a cash infusion, it would have drawn attention. Buying drinks for the house at a local pub, purchasing a new BMW, or plunking some of it down for an eighty-inch flat screen might have alerted someone that something fishy was going on. A cop spending a lot of money is often a cop that seized it illegally.

"So you moved on to what?"

"Vice," he laughed. "Can you believe that? I got into vice because I wanted to work on something clean. But busting hookers and perverts turned out to be less dirty than narcotics. At least I didn't have to look over my shoulder all the time."

"Did Ed finish his career in narcotics?" I asked.

"Nope," he replied. "That guy I mentioned, Kim Sponsler? He left narcotics pretty soon after I did, turns out he had a similar problem with what Ed was doing. Best way to get rid of the problem is to move on to another area, like I did. He actually moved up the ranks and became captain. And when he did, he instituted some new policies. Things got strict.

And Kim finally built a case against Ed and Jimbo."

"What happened to them?"

"Moved them out of narcotics. Onto desk jobs in the station. Just had to keep them away from the evidence locker."

"I imagine they weren't pleased with that," I said. "Took a hit on their bottom line."

"I'm sure it did. But the weird thing is, and I got this from one of the guys that used to work with them. They felt they were doing something noble all that time. Taking drug money from dealers. Putting them out of business. If the dealers owed any money to bigger dealers in their upline, they were in trouble. A few of those perps got killed. Others got out of Largo Beach fast, moved out of state. For Ed and Jimbo, that meant they were helping the community."

"Like Robin Hood. Except instead of giving to the poor, they were keeping the money for themselves."

"Yeah. Good way to put it. And eventually the two of them retired. Or I guess they took disability, that's how it's done a lot of times. But the way it was handled, quietly pushing them aside, yeah, it was probably for the best. Let them leave with some dignity. No need for a scandal."

I nodded. "So, in the end, Ed and his partner got away with it."

"Pretty much. All that money over the years. I don't know how he kept from bragging about what he did. That's what drags down a lot of guys. They have to tell people how smart they are. If you want to get away with something, the easiest route is keep your mouth shut."

"I wonder how that worked for Ed," I mused, recalling the

nice car he drove and the nice vacations he took his family on. Maybe that's why he lived in Culver City, far away from Largo Beach.

Sokolov shrugged and dipped some waffle into a puddle of syrup. "Didn't seem to pose a problem."

"Let me get back to why I'm here. Trying to figure out what happened with Ed's granddaughter, Amanda Zeal. Any ideas?"

"Hard to say. I still see Ed around once in a while, we both live in Culver City. He hasn't taken any hits over what he's done. But I'll tell you something. Karma's a real bitch. You never know how things even up. But they always seem to."

I frowned. Could Amanda's disappearance be some sort of cosmic answer to her grandfather's crimes? Things often did even up in life, in ways we usually never imagine. I thought of Gail and I thought of Marcus and I thought of whether any of the unsavory things I did for a living would come back and haunt them. I shuddered as I considered this.

*

I left Polly's with a stomach full of waffles and not much more. As I chugged onto the northbound 405 freeway, I decided that since I was headed toward home, a slight detour over to USC would not consume much more time. I had no idea if Amanda Zeal was hiding out at her brother's apartment, but I also had no idea of where else to look.

The Harbor Freeway turned out to be as gridlocked as the 405, and perhaps even more so. The traffic inched along, bumper-to-bumper all the way to Vernon, where I finally spun off onto surface streets and things moved a little bit quicker. I reached the USC Village, just north of campus at half-past seven, and after wasting fifteen minutes hunting for a parking space, I finally pulled into a red zone and crossed my fingers.

The apartments in the USC Village had just been erected a few years ago. A sprawl of gorgeous five-story mixed-use buildings began on the corner of Hoover and Jefferson and spread outward for many blocks. There was a wide, open-air plaza with a bell tower nearby, and a dining hall featuring stained glass and gothic-style seating. High-end restaurants came in. A Target and a Trader Joe's were built. The result was fifteen acres of loveliness sitting within a cradle of nearby poverty. Whereas this section of the extended campus had suffered numerous safety and crime issues for decades, it now gave the impression of something more akin to a college-town atmosphere, albeit one that came complete with a cappuccino bar and upscale shops. There was undoubtedly a Starbucks nearby, but I decided I had had my fill of caffeine for the moment.

I knocked on the door of Aaron Zellis's apartment, and then I knocked some more. At this hour, unless a college student was an unabashed morning person, the odds were good that they were fast asleep. I started pounding, which caused a few doors down the hallway to open, and a number of sleepy-eyed students wandered out, blinking and looking around to see what all the fuss was. One of them held a phone at the ready, perhaps to record a newsworthy event that might be valuable to share with the world. I flashed my badge and, without identifying myself as anything other than an important person, ordered them to go back inside their apartments. Most did, and rather quickly. Except for one.

"Hi," he said, looking more alert than most, but likely about twenty-five years old, and probably a graduate student. "I'm the building manager. What's wrong?"

"I need to find Aaron Zellis," I said in an official voice, glancing behind him to make sure there were no phones pointing in our direction. "Police business. You're the manager? I need you to unlock the door."

"Um, I don't think I can do that," he frowned.

"Do you want to go to jail this morning?" I said, giving him my best glower. "Because right now you're interfering with a criminal investigation. And you may be charged with aiding and abetting a felon."

"A felon? Aaron?" he said, trying to process this. "You're kidding."

"I'm not kidding and I don't have time to waste. If you don't open this door right now, there may be criminal charges filed," I declared, not bothering to clarify that right now, the only crime being committed was by me, impersonating a police officer.

"Okay, okay," he finally said and reached into his pocket for a set of keys. He fumbled with them until he settled on the proper key, slipped it into the deadbolt and unlocked the door. He pushed open the door and started to go inside, but I put a hand on his shoulder.

"That's all. I'll take it from here."

Nodding, he continued to look a bit confused, not entirely sure he was doing the right thing by following my orders, not entirely sure what other options were at his disposal. I entered the apartment and told him to go back to his own unit. I shut the door behind me and flipped the deadbolt closed to emphasize my point. I had briefly thought of ordering him not to say anything to anyone, but that alone might be enough to elevate his concerns to where he might actually go and say something to someone. Like the LAPD.

Aaron Zellis's living room was an unholy mess, the kind only a teenager could live through. There were clothes strewn here and there, and a half-eaten Taco Bell burrito supreme sitting atop a coffee table. Across from the table was a 60" flat-screen TV mounted to the wall. Five empty bottles of Bud Light sat haphazardly on the table, the sixth was lying on the floor. There was no sign that a girl had been here, and no sign that any girl would want to come here. I heard a rustling sound in the bedroom and a young man of about nineteen walked out. He was a good-looking kid, tall and well-built, with a mop of light blond hair. He had on a gray t-shirt and gray underwear, and was trying to focus on the stranger in his unit.

"Hello, Aaron," I said. "My name's Burnside and I need to talk with you. I'm working for your father."

"Oh yeah. My dad said he was hiring someone to look into what's going on with my sister."

I pointed to the couch and motioned for him to sit down. I walked into his bedroom and opened the closet. Nothing. I walked into the bathroom and peeked behind the shower curtain. Empty. If there were a fire escape I would have looked there, too, but there was none. Satisfied that Amanda wasn't in the apartment, but dissatisfied I was no closer to finding her, I walked back into the living room, picked up a dining room chair and plopped it down across from Aaron.

"You heard about what happened at Amanda's apartment building the other morning? About Moose Machado?" I asked.

"About Moose, sure," he said. "My dad told me. Plus, it was all over the news. That was messed up."

"Do you know where your sister is?"

"No, like I told Dad. I haven't heard from her in a week. She hasn't turned up?"

"She's still missing. Do you have any idea where she might possibly be?"

He shook his head. "No idea. She has her life, I have mine. Sounds like she's in some kind of trouble."

I scanned the empty beer bottles on his coffee table. "I don't know, Aaron. She was reportedly with Moose when he was killed, but she hasn't been seen since. I need to ask you a few questions. I apologize if this is coming off as brusque. But I need your help."

"Um. Okay."

"Do you know many of Amanda's friends?"

"Not so much anymore. I know she was seeing some guy from Fox. Wyatt, I think his name was."

"Okay. Let me ask you about Moose. What was Amanda's relationship like with him?"

Aaron Zellis continued to frown. "I don't know. Not exactly, anyway. They had a thing for a while, but that was when Amanda was younger. High school. I think she liked being with an older guy for some reason. I didn't like it, but it's not my life. Last few years they've mostly been friends, I guess."

"Odd friendship, don't you think? All things considered?"

"Yeah. Odd."

"What did they have in common?" I asked.

"Football," he replied without hesitating. "Moose played it, he knew a lot about the game. He helped Amanda out."

"Helped her out? How so? Like in prepping for her broadcasts?"

"Yeah, that. And also something else, I think."

"What?"

Aaron started to fidget. His eyes focused on the floor. I looked down there, too, and didn't see anything. I looked back up at him.

"Listen," I said, "your sister is very likely in some trouble. Anything you can tell me that might help find her would be good. You never how a small detail might turn out to be very important."

"Yeah," he started. "Okay. Well, you knew that Moose was a gambler."

"I did. Not a very good one, from what I understand."

"He had his ups and downs. But Amanda got interested in it. And last year they were winning some money on football games. Serious money."

"Okay," I said expectantly. "How were they doing it?"

Aaron took a breath, as if to work out what to say next. Finally, he spoke.

"She said they had some inside information. Tips. They knew things other people didn't."

I stared at him. Betting on sports was a common thing in America. Lots of people did it. I personally never liked gambling, and I viewed it as a waste of time and money.

Many bets involved point spreads and these could often be decided by a dropped pass, a deflected field goal attempt, or a fourth down conversion that came up just short. Football was indeed a game of inches, the winds of chance deciding a lot of wagers. But if someone had inside information, then that was a different story. Knowing a star player was injured, or learning some other hidden tidbit could be incredibly valuable. The problem was that these insider tips could rarely be confirmed, and lots of people lost huge sums following bad leads. But it sounded like Amanda and Moose might have had a more reliable source.

"How did they know this?"

"Someone told them," he responded and held up his hands. "I don't know who."

"Was it Moose or Amanda that had this source?"

"I think it was Amanda. Moose knew some bookies. Why they didn't just fly to Vegas and place the bets is beyond me."

I didn't say anything. If Amanda was getting inside information and using it to gamble, the network would fire her immediately. And if she were betting large sums of money, her winnings would be taxable if she did it at a legal sports book in Nevada. There were reasons people still used bookies, and there probably always would be.

"So she began doing well," I said, waiting for more.

"Yeah. She actually started to win a lot. She liked to joke that it was beginner's luck. I don't know if that actually exists."

"It doesn't exist," I said. "Especially not in gambling."

Beginner's luck was a misnomer. You sometimes see a rookie in pro sports or a freshman in college appear unstoppable at first. But in the following year, they often take a step back and aren't as terrific. Some people called that a sophomore slump. But it was really just that opposing teams had more game film, and someone diagnosed a good way to defend the player. Then all the other teams see that it's worked and they copy it. The freshman phenom stops being so phenomenal. That's when the hard work comes in for them to improve. If the beginner was at all lucky, it was simply because the other teams didn't know much about them.

"Doesn't the law of averages come into play here?" he asked.

"Yeah," I finally said. "But when most people start something new, they often have no fear. It allows them to take risks, and they usually do it in small increments. Once they start winning a little, they bet more and the stakes get higher. Not everyone handles the pressure well, and they start getting nervous. Beginner's luck isn't really luck. A lot of it is lack of fear."

"Okay."

"There's an explanation for everything," I said, starting to wonder if it was true in the Amanda Zeal case, and if I'd ever find out what that was.

"Yeah. But she was doing really well at first."

"And Moose?"

Aaron gave me an odd look. "He was just doing what Amanda was doing. If she was winning, he was winning. When she lost, he lost."

"Uh-huh," I said. "Let's back up a little. The more I look at your sister's background, the more incongruent it gets.

Grows up in Beverly Hills and has a good-paying job, but seems overly concerned with money. She's a beautiful girl, but she takes up with someone twice her age, a guy who's broke and doesn't have all that much going for him. And she seems to have gotten into a few physical altercations along the way. How does all that add up?"

"I don't know."

"Okay, but you're her brother. You must have some idea."

Aaron thought about this for a minute. "She's got some anger issues," he finally said. "I guess we both do. Divorce and all. Maybe she's a little self-destructive, I don't know. My girlfriend's a psych major we talk about this sometimes. Plus, Dad doesn't give us a lot. I mean, he pays for college, but like, he told me to get a part-time job to earn spending money. I started working at a frozen yogurt shop. I don't mind, but it's a little weird."

"How so?"

"Dad's got all this cash, but he hoards it. Thinks he needs to teach us about the real world, that we live in some kind of bubble because we grew up rich in Beverly Hills. We did, but he's the one who put us there. We were born into this. When I was seven, he enrolled me in karate classes. Did the same for Amanda when she was young. Told us never to take any crap from other kids. That's fine if you grew up in the hood, but it caused some problems for us along the way. Beverly Hills isn't the hood."

"Okay," I said, starting to wonder what lessons I was providing for Marcus. "How'd that work out?"

"I got into a lot of fights in school. Amanda got into a few, too. One time some guys were bothering me, she came over and punched one of them in the face. He was so shocked he didn't know what to do."

"And this is all because your father directed you to not take crap from anyone."

"Yeah. He wanted us to be able to take care of ourselves. Solve our own problems. We can, but, like I said, it led to bigger problems. I had to learn when to throw punches and when to walk away."

"Not a bad lesson to learn," I said. "Okay. Is there anything else you can tell me? Anything at all about Amanda? I'm really at the end here. I'm looking for her and there aren't a lot of avenues to go down. Any direction you can give would be helpful."

Aaron shrugged. "Not really. I have no idea. Now I'm a little worried."

I stood up and handed him my card, not bothering to tell him I was a little worried, too.

"I hope you find her," he managed. "None of this sounds good."

"No, it doesn't," I said, and walked out into the hall. There was one student waiting there for me. She turned on her phone and pointed it in my direction, recording my walk down the hall. I briefly thought of ripping the device out of their hands and throwing it against a wall. Ultimately, I decided that would accomplish little, other than to serve as an outlet for my total frustration at the pace with which this investigation was moving. As I walked downstairs and out of the building, all of that changed suddenly. I called Phil Zellis to give him an update. I got something entirely different.

"Burnside," he said, the background noise indicating he

was in his car. "I can't believe what just happened. I just got the call. I'm on my way over there now."

"What call? Over to where?" I asked.

"My father's house. Up on Culver Crest. The police just called me. There's been, a, well, a shooting, I guess. It's bad. They found him. My father. They found him in the house. He's dead."

Nine

The narrow street on Culver Crest felt even more congested with a half-dozen black-and-white SUVs parked there unevenly, a few still keeping their red and blue lights flashing. A number of plain black sedans were also nearby, indicating that the Culver City detective squad had arrived. I finally found a spot two blocks away and hiked up the street. A thuggish looking uniformed cop stood at the entrance of Ed Zellis's house, a bored expression on his pasty face. When I approached, his small eyes lit up.

"Hi there," I began, showing him my P.I. license. "I'm working for the family."

"Doing what?" he said, ignoring my license.

"Looking into the disappearance of a family member."

"Who?"

"The granddaughter," I said and pointed to the house. "The owner's granddaughter."

"Uh-huh. Come back some other time. This is a crime scene."

"Ah," I said, briefly considering asking a question about why there wasn't any yellow crime scene tape put up, like the way they always have it on TV. "Me thinks not."

He no longer looked bored, but rather, gave off the distinct impression he wanted to take me aside and work me over. An ugly sneer came across his lips. It did not improve his appearance.

"Take a walk, dude," he growled, and pointed to the street. "I'm not telling you again."

"Good," I said, feeling the impatience starting to boil over. "Because I don't want to hear it again. I have information that's related to this case. Police business. I'd like to speak with the detective heading up the investigation."

"Oh, you'd like that, huh?" he said, his sneer getting nastier.

"Yes, please. Pretty please. I hope I don't have to say it again for it to sink in."

"You may not have to. I may bounce you off that curb."

"I suppose you can try," I said, pretending to stifle a yawn. It was harder to do than I thought.

"I can do more than try, pal."

"You're not my pal. But if you want to try, I hope you took out that extra disability insurance. You may need it."

"Officer!" came a voice behind us. We turned to see a man in an ill-fitting brown suit wearing an unknotted rep striped tie, pulled halfway down his shirt. It was warm this morning, but it wasn't that warm.

"Yeah, Sarge?"

"Who is this guy?"

"Private dick. Says he's been working for the family."

"Is his name Burnside?"

The officer turned and looked at me. "Your name Burnside?"

"Last I checked."

He turned back to the detective. "Uh-huh."

"Bring him in here," the man in the brown suit ordered, and then he walked back into the house.

The officer gave a sigh and glared at me. He moved his chin toward the front door, an exercise that barely took any effort. He didn't move out of my way, but neither did he give any indication I was welcome. I wondered if he would still be here on my way out.

Ed Zellis's home looked roughly the same as it did a few days ago. The marvelous city view was still visible through the wall of glass in the living room. The only thing different was that the living room was now loaded with cops, and a dead body was now lying under a sheet, about ten feet away from the burgundy recliner. Phil Zellis was sitting on the recliner, but he was not leaning back. Rather, he was bent forward, staring down at the shag carpet. His mouth was tight and his eyes were intense.

"Hi Phil," I said, walking up to him. "Sorry for your loss."

"Burnside," he said in a low voice. "Thanks for coming. Any word on Amanda?"

"Not yet," I told him. "I still have a few leads to chase down, but I haven't caught up with her."

"This is horrible," he said, picking up his head and looking out the window. "Dad never should have involved himself in this mess with Amanda."

I gaped at him. "How did he get involved?"

"Someone called him yesterday, said they had kidnapped his granddaughter. Wanted a ridiculous amount of ransom money. Dad told me he was going to find Amanda on his own. Said he was the best detective around and he was going to mess up the people who took her."

I shuddered at this. There's an old saying that a lawyer who represents himself in court has a fool for a client. The same logic applies here. An investigator who looks into a personal matter involving family often does not think clearly. Their emotions are raw and they are often unleashed. No matter how good a detective might be or might have been, they can't be impartial and they are prone to make mistakes. They had a vested interest in the outcome, and things could boil over in a hurry. That Ed was likely pushing seventy years old made the issue even more problematic.

"So he went and tried to find Amanda on his own?"

"Dad said he had a plan. He didn't tell me what it was."

At that point, the detective in the brown suit approached and wagged his index finger at me. He walked to the other side of the living room. I patted Phil on the shoulder and followed him across the room.

"I'm Detective Gottschalk. I'm leading this investigation."

I nodded and tried to look impressed.

"What's your role here? Burnside, is it?"

"Right. Ed's son Phil brought me in. Phil's daughter Amanda and her boyfriend were assaulted earlier this week. Side street in Beverly Hills. Phil then hired a friend, Anthony Machado, as a bodyguard for her. The next day Machado gets killed in the garage of Amanda's building. Then Amanda disappears."

"You find out what happened?"

"Nope."

Gottschalk raised his eyebrows. "You end up doing *anything* this week? Aside from collecting what's probably a healthy fee?"

I rolled that around for a minute, and started to get annoyed. "Yeah, actually I did do something. I found out that Amanda and Machado had a thing once. And Amanda had a carefree lifestyle and hung out with pro football players. And they both had a gambling problem, the biggest problem being they were losing a lot of money. I also learned Ed was a crooked cop down in Largo Beach. And Phil has a problem with marrying too many women. I found out the L.A. City Attorney is corrupt. I also found out that waffles taste a lot better with maple syrup than without."

"The City Attorney?" he frowned. "Sutker? He's running for mayor, isn't he?"

"Not for long," I said, casually.

"How do you know all this?"

"I do my job thoroughly," I said, thinking in the back of my mind that I still hadn't come up with answers to the questions I was paid to get answers for. I also wondered how much of what Arthur Woo told me about Jay Sutker I should be sharing. But I was getting to the point where I didn't care much about who knew what. There were now two people found dead the day after I'd spoken to them, and the leads were spurious.

"Thorough, huh?" he muttered. "All right. What do you make of this?"

I looked around the living room. "Was a weapon found?"

"Nope. Nothing nearby."

"That rules out a suicide," I mused.

"Yeah, we've already gotten that far. Crooked cop, you say? Well, crooked or not, who'd want to kill a retired officer from a city thirty miles away?"

"I don't know. In fact, Ed's career in Largo Beach may or may not be directly related to what happened here. But cops who are dirty often have other skeletons rattling around in their closet. Take a look around. This seem like the house that a retired cop would own? I heard he had a curious departure from Largo Beach. Took disability, wound up getting an awfully nice severance package."

"Doesn't mean anything. Lots of cops end their careers like that."

I nodded. But when someone broke the rules on one thing, they often broke the rules on other things. Once they crossed the line and gave up their values, it was easy to keep sidestepping the boundaries whenever it suited them. The rules became nothing more than an inconvenience, or in some cases, a challenge to overcome.

"So how was he crooked?" Gottschalk asked. "Was he on the take?"

"No. He was ripping off drug dealers. Busting them, but some of their stash and most of their money never found their way to the evidence locker. Ed wound up living a nice lifestyle," I said, gesturing to the living room.

"Okay. Probably not a perfect guy, but I've seen worse. You think any of those drug dealers might have come up here seeking revenge?"

"I don't know," I said, starting to wonder if any of Ed's

collars might have gotten released from prison recently. The timing of that, however, seemed like it might be awfully coincidental, given everything else that had happened this week.

"Right, you don't know. Okay. Tell me about the granddaughter. Amanda, you say? She's the one that seems to be connected with all of this."

"Yeah, Amanda Zeal."

"And she disappeared after the bodyguard was killed."

"Yeah."

"And the boyfriend? He have a name?"

I shrugged. "Wyatt Angstrom. The Beverly Hills PD is looking into him."

"Uh-huh," Gottschalk said. "Funny thing. We checked Ed Zellis's phone. He's had a number of calls with this Wyatt Angstrom the past couple of days. Mostly short, a minute or two. Know what they might have been talking about?"

I frowned at the revelation. "No idea. I spoke with Drew Slick yesterday, he's the lead detective in Beverly Hills. They haven't been able to make contact with Angstrom. Said something about getting a warrant to search his apartment."

Gottschalk sniffed. "A warrant? Hmmph. Leave it to Beverly Hills to do everything by the book. Okay, I'll talk to Slick. Lots of pieces to turn over in this one. So the deceased was looking into the granddaughter disappearing. Tell me about her."

"Amanda Zeal. She's an on-air reporter for Fox. Works the sidelines during football games."

"Good looking?"

"Oh, yeah."

"Maybe a stalker involved?"

I thought back to what Moose had told me a few days ago. "I heard she's had a few of those in her past, so you can't rule it out. But my sixth sense tells me no. As I said, she and her boyfriend were assaulted on the street. Haven't found out by whom or the reason why, but there are plenty of people around who had problems with her."

"Like who?"

"People she worked with weren't crazy about her. Neither were some of the fans. The coaches she harangued on the sideline got annoyed with her. She had a thing with a few players, too. Didn't end well."

"Yeah, you mentioned that," he asked, raising his eyebrows. "Don't have to go further than football players to find a bunch of violent guys."

I frowned. "Maybe."

"Need some names."

I turned my head and looked out the crystal clear window. The view was as marvelous as ever. I thought about Xavier and Rhett, and didn't like the idea of passing their names along to law enforcement. I also didn't like the idea of two dead bodies who had loose associations to me, and ultimately to them. I wondered if either player was capable of murder, or why they'd pick Amanda's grandfather. I doubted Xavier had any lingering issue with Amanda. And while Rhett certainly did, he didn't strike me as the type who would go out seeking vengeance.

"You can't have them," I finally said.

"And why not?"

"It's confidential."

"Oh, it's confidential, huh? Maybe we just run you in for obstructing justice."

"Won't matter. You can toss me in the can, but eventually you'll have to release me. And then you'll have a civil suit on your hands. But you still won't have the names."

"You're a real wise guy," he glared.

"I've been called worse. But I promise you this. If anything turns up regarding these players, I'll call you right away."

Gottschalk sighed. "So Phil's got some women problems, huh?"

I peered at him. "Phil's on his third marriage," I said. "My guess is he'll be on his way to the fourth soon."

"That have anything to do with Ed?"

"Doubt it, but I guess you never know."

"Have anything to do with Amanda?"

I stared at him for a long minute. "I don't know."

"You seem to know a lot about some things. But nothing that does us any good here."

I averted my eyes and focused on the shag carpet. "Sad, but true," I agreed.

*

I spent another half hour talking with Gottschalk and then one other detective before they said they had all they needed. I asked Phil to call me later in the day. I walked out of Ed Zellis's house and looked both ways for the thuggish-looking cop with the pasty face, but he wasn't nearby. I decided not to wait for him, and gave some thought to just what it was I'd do next.

It was almost ten now and getting warm. I tried to figure out why Phil hadn't told me about the kidnapping and the ransom, but all I managed to do was give myself a headache. I called Drew Slick and learned his people had indeed spoken with Wyatt Angstrom, but they learned little. They felt Angstrom acted suspiciously, but they couldn't hold him just for that. I told him about Ed Zellis and Aaron and my breakfast in Largo Beach, but Detective Slick didn't express much interest.

After I hung up, I imagined the problems of trying to bring together multiple crimes in multiple jurisdictions. The city of Los Angeles spreads out from the port in San Pedro up through West L.A. and into the San Fernando Valley. But the greater Los Angeles region spreads out much further. It is a patchwork of communities, and there are nooks and crannies like Beverly Hills, Culver City, and Santa Monica that have their own municipalities, usually with their own police forces. Other cities like West Hollywood contract with the L.A. County Sheriff for law enforcement. The different agencies sometimes work together on things, but territorial issues introduce complications. I wondered if there was a way to uncomplicate them.

My old friend Juan Saavedra was in the process of transitioning from heading up LAPD's Westside Division to a new position at the downtown headquarters. I called and asked Juan if he was busy this morning. He snorted his reply.

The LAPD had been stationed for many decades at Parker Center. But Parker Center had been a flash point of controversy in the community, a symbol of the old style of policing that alienated many residents in the inner city. That some of these residents were actual criminals was immaterial. The LAPD brass decided their image needed an overhaul, and a few years ago they moved into an award-winning architectural masterpiece on First Street, just south of City Hall.

Once I weaved through their security protocol downstairs, it took me a while to find Juan's office. Only I didn't find Juan. An admin nearby told me he was in a meeting. I waited for about an hour, mostly thinking up ways a defense could stop the Rams' potent offense. Not many ideas came to mind. I felt my eyes begin to close.

"Well, looky here," finally came a voice from behind me. I turned to see Juan Saavedra looking very dapper in a navy suit, white shirt and maroon ivy league tie. His gray hair was freshly cut, and he projected the look of a professional politician more than a police officer.

I stood up and shook his hand. "You're looking like a newly promoted man," I said.

"Got to dress for success," he beamed and then sat down behind his desk.

"Is this how commanders dress?" I asked.

Juan still smiled. "The whole idea is you dress for the job you want, not the job you have."

"Smart. You're moving up in the world," I said, knowing I had played a role. When I helped crack the Tyler Briggs case recently, the deputy chief in charge of the detective bureau, Larry Herzog, was publicly humiliated. He had mishandled the Briggs investigation, and Juan was able to delicately remind the chief of a few other missteps Herzog had made.

Soon afterward, the deputy chief was reassigned to Special Projects, which was a nice way of telling him to retire, or else.

"Remember Kevin Perlow? He was commander in charge of detective services, but with Herzog on the outs, he got a bump up to deputy chief. Someone needed to replace Kevin's position. Guess that someone's going to be me."

"Nice."

Juan leaned back in his overstuffed leather chair. "Well, the wife's happy about my raise. My oldest is applying to Princeton. He's a straight-A student, the college counselor thinks he'll get in. Hey, you know how much higher education costs nowadays?"

"Oh, yeah. You recall I was a college football coach not too long ago."

"I swear. Over seventy grand. Every year for four years. He'll probably get some financial aid, he'll have to. I can't afford all that on my own," Juan said, his voice getting a little sad. "But if he's got his heart set on Princeton, we'll find a way to get him there."

"That's what happens when you sign on as a parent. You're supposed to sacrifice for your kids."

"Heck, my dad threw me out of the house when I was eighteen. Said sink or swim. I learned to swim. But it's harder today. A lot harder."

"Very astute," I remarked. "The world's changing."

"Yeah," he said and gave a sly smile. "But we still got crooks around here. That's why we both have jobs. I'm going to miss running the Westside. The only benefit of downtown is I get to go to El Tepeyac occasionally."

I remembered El Tepeyac from a brief stint I did at the LAPD Hollenbeck station in East L.A., which was located nearby. The restaurant was a cop favorite, especially after the owner created a dish in honor of the local police, who asked for a burrito with as many ingredients as possible thrown into it.

"Haven't been there in a while. They still have those oversized burritos?"

"Ha! Yeah. I got to watch it though. Have too many of those I'm going to need to have my nice pants let out at the waist," he said, patting his stomach and then looking over at me. "So, I take it this isn't just a visit to congratulate me."

I gave a small smile back. "You know me. Give a little to get a little."

"So what's going on?"

"I started off looking into an assault case. Turned into a double homicide, one in Beverly Hills, the other in Culver City. One of the victims was a former detective down at Largo PD. Name's Ed Zellis. Ed's granddaughter was involved in the original assault."

"Victim or perp?" Juan asked.

"I started off thinking she's the victim. Now I'm not real sure."

"Uh-huh."

"I'm trying to pull all this together and not getting far. The granddaughter's disappeared, not sure if it's by her choice or not."

"Interesting. I suppose I come in at some point here."

"Well, maybe. I'd like to talk with Chief Bates."

Juan stared at me for a long moment, his face looking

incredulous. Then he started to laugh. "You want me to set up a meeting. Just you and the chief."

"Well, I suppose you could be there, too." I offered.

"Big of you. Mind telling me what you want from Chief Bates?"

"Ed Zellis played poker with the chief. I thought maybe he could give me some insight into who might want to bump him off."

"Ah," Juan said, the smile still evident on his face but fading quickly. "What a great idea. Have you grill the LAPD chief of police on what he knew about a stiff. Maybe we should set you up in a room with a single light bulb and a rubber hose to work him over if he doesn't come clean. That good with you?"

"Well, we may not need to take it to extremes."

"No, we may not indeed. Look, Burnside. We've known each other for a long time. And we've done each other some favors. One hand washes the other and all that. But I don't get a whole lot of face time with the chief myself. And the last thing I'm going to do is ask him to do a sit-down with a P.I. who got kicked off the force ten years ago. No offense, mind you."

"None taken," I said.

"Look, I don't like the idea of any of our brothers getting taken down, retired or not, Largo Beach or wherever. Us cops take care of our own. But there's some office politics I have to be sensitive to here. If there's some other angle I can help you with, we'll see. But we're dealing with two murders in two different jurisdictions. It's hard enough for those two departments, Beverly and Culver, to work together. Throw

LAPD into the mix? I don't think so."

"Okay. I hear you," I said. I wasn't disappointed, nor was I surprised. But it never hurts to ask.

"Anything else I can say no to? Since I'm in such a good mood and all?"

"I guess asking you to call up Largo PD and get a list of Ed Zellis's collars over the years might be a bit much to ask," I said.

"Just a bit. You know anyone down there?"

"Yeah. I had a plate of waffles with one of their detectives this morning. Didn't think he'd be receptive to my asking him for a favor. One that included a lot of extra work."

"So glad you felt comfortable asking me." Juan said. "But you know something. You might just go down to their library. They won't have police records. But they might have old issues of the local newspaper saved. If you're lucky they'll be digitized. If you're not, you'd have to look at a lot of years worth of microfiche."

"Microfiche," I repeated, dreading the idea of spending hours chasing down what might end up being a dead end. "Haven't used that in, oh, a couple of decades. Say, let me ask you something else."

Juan sighed. "Listening."

"Anything you can tell me about a Wyatt Angstrom? He's going out with the granddaughter."

"If it'll get you out of here quicker, well, okay," he said.

Turning to his computer, Juan asked me to spell the last name. He spent a few minutes looking through some databases. Finally, something caught his attention.

"He reported his car stolen a few months ago. White

Jaguar. Said someone stole it out of the Fox lot on Pico. From the garage. Never recovered."

"Okay. Anything else on Wyatt?"

"Let's see. Well. Got busted for check washing ten years ago, but the jury failed to convict."

"Oh?" I said.

"Yeah. And then there's this. He did get convicted of tax evasion a couple of years ago."

"Really? I guess those monthly Jaguar payments. Must have needed the cash. He do any time in the can?"

"Says here he got no jail time, just a slap on the wrist," Juan commented, shaking his head. "I hate this crap. Some people think tax fraud is a victimless crime. Non-violent offender and all. They say leave the prisons for the hardened criminals. Problem is, guys like this just keep doing what they're doing. Half of them will go before a judge again on the same charge. Might get a longer probation. Not much impetus to change their behavior if the punishment isn't there."

"Yeah," I said, starting to wonder what else Wyatt had been up to that he had been getting away with. It might be time to pay him another visit.

"If we're going to have laws, we ought to enforce 'em," Juan continued. "Convict these felons and put 'em away. My two cents, anyway. Hey, speaking of convicting people. How's everything by Gail? Still keeping busy prosecuting bad guys?"

"She's fine," I said.

"I guess she'll be getting a new boss next year. Sutker's taking a run at mayor."

"He'll lose," I said. "There'll be some dirt coming out on Sutker soon."

"That's interesting," he said approvingly. "Got any more gossip?"

I decided to choose my words carefully. "Maybe her new boss will be the good citizens of Los Angeles."

Juan squinted at me. "Say what?"

"Gail's thinking of running for City Attorney. Doing more than thinking actually. We've started looking into fundraising."

Juan let out a low whistle. "Well, I'll be. You might end up as a political spouse."

"I might."

"And knowing Gail," he said slowly, pondering this for a moment, "she could have quite a career in politics. Good-looking, smart, articulate. She's got the whole package. You might be First Man one day."

"Not likely. I have some baggage. The whole thing concerns me. I don't want her to get labeled because of something I was accused of a decade ago. And falsely, I should add."

Juan nodded. "True. Being a public servant takes its toll. More on the families than on the person themselves. And you've got your past history."

"There's that."

"Worried about anything else?" he asked.

"I think I've got enough on my plate right now to worry about, thanks."

"Okay. And keep me informed about what's going on with that case of yours. I like keeping tabs on you."

"And the chief probably likes keeping tabs on what cases the PDs like Beverly Hills and Culver City and Santa Monica are working on," I said.

"He does."

"And he'll have you to thank for the info. And the gossip."

"He will."

I got up to leave, albeit unsure of where to go to next. "Glad I could be of service to you."

Juan stood up and shook my hand. "Glad you could be of service to me, too."

Ten

Driving back to the Westside, I called Drew Slick and told him to expect to hear from a Culver City detective named Gottschalk. I asked him if he had talked to Wyatt Angstrom and he told me they had finally found him at the studio, but had failed to learn much. Angstrom hadn't been back to his apartment, so they had gone inside. After tossing the place, Slick said he came across an unregistered handgun, which was passed on to ballistics. The initial finding was that it did not appear to have been fired recently, and it was clearly a different caliber than the gun used to killed Moose. They had no other leads on the case, and finding Amanda Zeal was one of many things on Slick's to-do list. It did not strike me this was an urgent matter for him. I decided it was urgent for me.

I headed for the Fox lot on Pico. The security guard who flagged me down asked for my name, but I told him I wouldn't be on anyone's list. He dramatically removed his mirrored sunglasses and started to launch into his stump speech about no one being admitted without being on the sacred list, but I short-circuited his lecture by flashing my fake badge. He stopped talking and I grabbed that moment to remind him that the penalty for interfering with law enforcement was time in the state penitentiary. He stared at me for a second and then let me go through without further discussion. I didn't bother pulling into the garage, but rather slid my Pathfinder into a parking space with an executive's name painted on the asphalt.

I headed up to the sixth floor, passing a multitude of workers headed in the opposite direction, undoubtedly going to lunch. Wyatt Angstrom's office door was open and I breezed past Dirk, who tried in vain to play traffic cop, but I ordered him to back off in no uncertain terms. I was running out of patience, it showed, and I didn't care. When he started to protest, I shut the door in his face.

"Burnside?" Wyatt exclaimed, glancing up from what looked like a report summarizing last night's Nielsen ratings. "What's the meaning of this?! You can't just barge in here!"

"I just did. Where's Amanda?"

"I don't know," he yelled. "Don't you think I'd go get her if I knew?"

"What were you and Ed Zellis talking about?"

Wyatt Angstrom slammed the report down and stood up. He glared at me angrily. I looked into his intense eyes for a few seconds; one eye still looked pretty red. I noticed the marks on his face had barely begun to heal.

"I don't have to tell you anything!"

"You're doing a bang-up job of it," I said.

Angstrom stormed around his desk and pointed a finger

in my face. "You better watch your mouth," he declared. "I'm getting a little tired of this."

"Me, too."

With that, he grabbed my left arm and tried to pull me toward the door. I jerked my arm away, and then I hauled off and shoved him hard in the chest. He stumbled backward, a look of shock on his face. I shoved him hard again and got much the same reaction. I wanted to get his attention, and I did. And I also wanted to show who was in charge right now. It wasn't him.

"What the hell?!" he exclaimed, blinking a few times, his breath starting to heave. "What on earth did you do that ... "

This time I grabbed him by his button-down shirt and threw him against a wall. He began to get flustered, as if he didn't know what to do next. I then yanked his face inches from mine.

"Now you listen to me and listen good. I'm tired of this crap. You know something and you're not telling me. I'm not leaving here until I get some answers from you. If I have to hang you out the window by your ankles, so be it."

"Okay, okay," he whined. "Let me go."

I released my grip, but I shoved him again to let him know his reprieve would be brief if he didn't start cooperating. My right hand moved to the left side of my waist in case I needed to pull out my weapon. But Wyatt Angstrom was not about to ratchet things up to the next level.

"Geez," he panted. "You didn't have to do that."

"Yeah, I know I didn't have to, but I did. Where's Amanda?"

"Honest," he said, holding his hands up. "I really don't

know."

I took a breath. It was always possible he was telling the truth. "Okay. Let's talk about what you do know. You and Ed had a bunch of phone conversations lately. Tell me what you talked about."

Wyatt hesitated, so I shoved him once more. I saw him flinch and pull back. "Okay, okay. It's about Amanda. She's been taken."

"By whom?" I asked.

"This group of guys. Gangbangers."

"Keep going,"

"These guys we owe money to. For gambling."

"Gambling on what?" I asked.

"Football games. She had an in. Tips. We were doing really well in the beginning of the season. Then not so much. We started losing. Amanda decided the best way to get whole was to bet more."

"Not smart," I said. "Not smart at all."

"Yeah, well, we know that now."

"You were betting, too?"

"Not as much as her. She was in deep, a good fifty large."

"Where were they getting their tips from?"

"Ed."

I stared at him and tried to piece this together in my mind. Nothing fit. "And why were you speaking with Ed so much yesterday?"

"Trying to work out how to get Amanda back."

"So you, Moose and Amanda owed these guys a lot of money. Why'd they kill Moose?"

"I don't know. I think maybe he got in the way when they

were going for Amanda. Moose wasn't worth much."

"You've got a funny way of placing value on human life."

"No, listen, I'm not making this stuff up. Look, if they grab Moose, no one cares. If they grab Amanda, they know she has access to money. Her father, her grandfather, maybe Fox corporate, too, who knows. They might pay to get her back. No one's paying for Moose."

I stepped back and looked at him. Kidnapping was a dumb crime, but criminals are rarely the best and the brightest, and they didn't often think things through carefully.

"But why didn't they go to Phil? He's Amanda's dad, and he owns a mansion in Beverly Hills. He's got more money than Ed. More money than most people."

"Phil said no."

I stared at him. "He said no to getting his daughter back?"

"He felt they were bluffing. Phil said they had no choice but to set her free. If he didn't pay, then killing Amanda would be pointless, because then they'd never get their fifty grand."

I rolled my eyes at the logic. "Did anyone think to call the police? Or the FBI? We're talking about a serious crime here, by some serious bad guys."

"The kidnappers said they'd kill Amanda if we brought in law enforcement, or even if we told anyone about it. They also said they'd hunt all of us down and kill the lot of us. After Moose, no one wanted to call their bluff. These are some really messed up dudes."

"So Phil said no. How does Ed get involved?"

"Ed called me after Amanda got taken, he said he was going to investigate. He wanted information, everything I knew about these people. I guess he made contact with them. He was going to go see them yesterday."

"Was he going to pay them?"

"I don't think so. He said he was going to put them away. And teach them a lesson."

I shook my head. Ed had to have been almost seventy. At a certain point, no matter how tough a guy is, no matter how smart, no matter how cunning, advanced age has a way of frittering all of that away. You're not as sharp, not as quick, and the things you were once good at don't come as easily. In some fields like medicine, people could have careers well into their eighties. For other fields, like football, most players' careers don't go beyond age thirty. For everyone else, the sweet spot is somewhere in between.

"Was Ed gambling on games, too?"

"Yeah, but I think he had his own bookie. And I don't think he was doing it at the level Amanda was."

"Then where'd Ed get these tips?"

"I think he knew a few refs. One of them may have been shaving points. At least that's what Amanda and I figured out. We had our doubts in the beginning, but then we saw the tips were paying off most of the time. Until they weren't."

I gave a sigh. This was among the worst possible scenarios a former athlete or coach could hear. You played the game hard and you played it honestly. You encouraged your players to do so as well. If everybody gave one hundred percent and they did their jobs right, then good things happen. But refs were human and there would always be the occasional blown call. A penalty flag thrown late in the game. Or conversely, a penalty the other team actually committed, but no flag was thrown because the refs didn't see it. The net result was your team was unable to finish what should have been a game-winning drive. We usually chalk that up to human error on the part of the ref. No one wanted to believe it could be anything more sinister.

"The Beverly Hills police finally talked to you."

"Yeah. Why?"

"I guess you haven't been around much."

"Can you blame me? Ever since Amanda and I got attacked the other night, I've been nervous. Stayed away from home. I checked into a hotel."

Maybe with good reason, I thought. "I take it you haven't heard about Amanda's grandfather."

"No. He was supposed to call this morning, but I never heard from him."

"He's dead," I told him. "The maid found his body a few hours ago."

The look of shock on Angstrom's face seemed genuine, the type of blank, confused look one has when they encounter something they were wholly unprepared for and could never have rehearsed. There were curious pieces to Angstrom's story, why he was laying low, and what his place might have been in all this. His role in the gambling ring was unsavory and illegal. But one thing seemed clear. Whatever he had been planning, murder did not seem to have been a part of it.

"What happened to Ed?" he finally managed.

"Gunshot wound to the head, looks like it's a homicide. Probably in his home, although he could have been shot somewhere else and they moved the body. But that's a lot of effort to go through, lugging a body around, don't you think?"

Angstrom nodded blankly in agreement. I watched him for a beat and continued.

"So Ed told you he was going to meet up with the guys who took Amanda."

"Yeah, that's what he said."

"He tell you anything about them?"

"Not much. Just that they lived in Compton."

I stared at him. "Compton," I repeated. "He tell you an address?"

"No," he said, but then Wyatt Angstrom's head perked up. "But I do remember something else. He said the guy he was meeting was named Alex. He likes to call himself Ax. That mean anything to you?"

*

Leaving the Fox lot, I drove down Pico and deliberated on how best to proceed. There were now multiple cities involved in this case, one homicide in Beverly Hills, and another in Culver City. A former Largo Beach detective had been murdered, and all roads pointed to Compton, another independent city woven into the chaotic fabric that is southern California. The only connection to Los Angeles was that the other homicide victim, Moose Machado, lived in a downtown apartment.

For a brief moment, I thought of contacting a detective at one of these local police departments, but I sensed that would be problematic. Compton no longer had its own police force; it was served by the L.A. County Sheriff's department, which was almost as bureaucratic as the LAPD. When a kidnapping occurs and someone is being held against their will, any wait time, even to coordinate resources was not advisable. This was one of the biggest problems with bureaucracies. Red tape caused delays and delays did not lead to good things. We could not show up too late. There is nothing worse than being too late.

I could have simply driven down to Compton by myself, but there were inherent dangers to that. I was dealing with a lethal person, or worse, a lethal group. Times like these made me wish I had a partner to back me up. But admittedly, these times were the exception. Good partnerships were rare in my business because they required a level of trust and a level of competence. Partners picked up half the money but they did not always pick up half the workload. And in the private investigator field, the quality of the investigators varied wildly. Even factoring in the number of former cops, there were often good reasons they no longer wore a shield, and there could be dire consequences if they failed to handle themselves properly. But still, there was safety in numbers.

As I hashed this over in my mind, I was jolted back into the present by the buzzing of my phone. It was as if the universe noticed me rolling this case around in my brain and sent someone to help me. Phil Zellis was on the line. He asked me to come over. It took me twenty minutes.

"Burnside," he said, opening the door quickly after I knocked. He stood there rigid, his breathing heavy as he clenched and unclenched his fists.

"Phil. How are you holding up?"

"Okay. I think the shock has worn off. I'm more angry

than anything."

"Angry?" I asked.

"Amanda's still gone. Wyatt's been worthless. I'm angry with Dad for jumping into this mess when he shouldn't have. You name it. Everything about this week has been rotten. Nothing's been uncovered about what happened to Moose. The Culver City cops don't have any leads on Dad. Feels like they're going to move as slow on this as Beverly Hills did on Moose."

"So you knew Amanda's been kidnapped," I said.

"I knew. And it stinks. I can't put my finger on it, but this feels all wrong."

"They contacted you for ransom."

"Yesterday. They wanted five hundred thousand dollars. I said no. I don't believe in negotiating with kidnappers, terrorists, you name it. You give in once, they'll take you again and again."

"What's their move now?" I asked.

There was a pause. "I don't know," he said.

I thought about how best to pose the next question. It was something I had been mulling over on the drive to Phil's. There was good and bad to involving Phil. He knew how to handle himself, but his emotions were raw. I started to think that might be exactly what I needed here. I also started to think I didn't have any other options, and time was not on our side.

"What if I told you I think I know where Amanda might be at. Want to take a spin?"

Phil's eyes raged. "You know where she is?"

"Maybe. Not certain. But it's worth a shot. One thing you

have to promise is to try and keep your emotions in check. Follow my lead. Back me up. Do what I say and you should be fine. Think you can manage that?"

Phil's answer did not come in the form of a verbal reply. Instead, he strode purposefully out the door and slammed it behind him.

"Let's roll," he said.

Compton was located just below South-Central L.A., and for many years had earned a notorious reputation for urban decay. Up until the 1960s, Compton was a middle-class black city, but when nicer homes in Baldwin Hills began attracting African-Americans, Compton fell into a steep decline. Crime-ridden for decades, the city began to right itself a few years ago. It disbanded its police department for excessive corruption, and it struck a deal where law enforcement would be handled by the county sheriff. It was far from a good area, but at least the decline seemed to have been stymied.

Traffic was moderate, and it took us half an hour on the Largo Beach Freeway to get to the Rosecrans exit and head west. We arrived at the address on Orchard Street that Alex Solis had generously provided me during our call, one that was only yesterday. It seemed like a week ago. We came upon a faded pink house on a quiet, sun-drenched street. The houses on the block were small, and all of them had gates or fencing surrounding what passed for front lawns. Bars covered all of the windows. The grass, what little of it there was, looked depressingly brown. But a shiny new white van with the name Star Rentals on it sat in front of the home where Alex Solis told me he lived, the van looking distinctly out of place.

A young man of about twenty years old sat on the curb in front of the house. He had a swarthy face and a bored expression. A three-inch scar ran along the skin above his jawbone. He wore a white t-shirt and had on a blue Dodgers baseball cap. In his hand was a large bottle of Olde English 800 beer. He did not make any effort to hide it, not even to slip it inside of a brown paper bag. Clearly, he didn't care what people thought, but there simply weren't many people around. We got out of the car and approached him.

"We're looking for Alex Solis," I told him in my most authoritative manner.

The young man gave us a bored look and took another sip of his beer. "What you want with him?" he asked.

"We want to ask him a few questions," Phil said, not bothering to follow my lead.

"About what?"

"That's between him and us," Phil continued.

"Why don't you ask me. I'll give him the message."

"Why don't you get off your butt and go find Alex."

The young man stood. "Why don't you go fuck yourself, *cochon*."

Phil stalked over and slapped the beer out of his hand. The bottle broke, and golden liquid splattered along the front walk. Some of it got on Phil's pants, but he didn't seem to notice. He grabbed the young man by the front of his t-shirt, but the man broke his grasp and punched Phil in the face with a quick left-right-left combination. Phil staggered for a moment before regaining his balance and unleashing a hard left hook to the temple, and the man fell to one knee.

"Oh, you're gonna pay for that, you *gringo* fuck," he sneered, and all of a sudden another man came out of nowhere.

The new guy leaped onto Phil's back, but before he could do anything, I grabbed him by the scruff of his neck and flung him to the ground. He jumped right back up, but I hit him with a back punch to the mouth which sent him reeling. By this time, the young man with the beer had gotten to his feet and was trying to box Phil, but not getting anywhere. Phil blocked two punches and then hit him solidly in the jaw. I was beginning to feel good about middle age being able to handle youth when I saw something out of the corner of my eye. The young man I had sent to the ground had gotten up again, but this time he had a pistol in his hand. He pointed it at us and yelled something unintelligible. Phil must have heard it, too. Everything came to a standstill.

"You two start walking," he yelled, waving the pistol wildly. We began to walk toward the Pathfinder and he yelled again. "No!" He pointed to the garage behind the house.

"Wait a minute," I said, not liking this at all.

"No, you wait a minute, motherfucker! Do as I say or I bust a cap in your *gabacho* ass. Get in there now!"

The first guy we had encountered, the one with the beer and the long scar, grabbed Phil by the arm and started to lead him toward the side of the house. I looked at the one with the pistol, who motioned me to follow. Scarface led us down a narrow, choppy driveway that had probably last been paved about sixty years ago, and was strewn with cracks. An old Chevy Impala with dents in both passenger-side doors sat at the end of the driveway. We moved into what was once a backyard but now held what might generously be called a guest house. A more accurate description would be a clubhouse for gangbangers.

Keeping the pistol trained on us, the man opened the door and motioned for us to go inside. There were half a dozen young men loitering about, one smoking a cigarette, two sipping cans of beer, another lying on a couch taking a nap. And then there was Amanda Zeal, her blonde hair flowing freely, sitting on a folding chair, staring at us.

"Hey, look what I caught snooping around," shouted our new friend with the gun. "Couple o' lawbreakers!"

"Oh, yeah?" said the guy with the cigarette, who seemed like he was the leader of this crew. He wore a black shirt, tan shorts, and he had an acne problem. He was overweight, and his head was almost perfectly round. The closer we got, the more the acne stood out. The complexion of his face was not unlike a pile of chopped meat.

"Caught 'em outside," Scarface said. "Snooping around."

The leader laughed and waved his cigarette at us. "Lawbreakers, huh?"

"Hey, you know what we do with lawbreakers," declared another, as he made a slicing motion across his throat.

"What you bitches trying to steal?" asked the guy with the cigarette. We did not respond.

"Hey, baby," said the guy standing next to us with the gun, as he looked at Amanda. "You know these clowns?"

Amanda Zeal continued to stare at us, mouth open. Her hands were at her side, and it didn't appear she was tied up. But she clearly didn't look like she wanted to be there.

"What's a matter, baby? Cat got your tongue?"

The guy with the gun walked over to me and put the gun flush against my left temple. The gun felt cold and hard against my head. My breathing slowed as I tried to keep calm and process the situation. A trickle of sweat rolled down my rib cage.

"That's my dad," she finally managed. "And a friend of his."

"Oh, that's Daddy, huh?" said the guy with the cigarette, as he took a puff. "The man with the big bank account. Who don't care if his daughter lives or dies. I got that straight, Daddy?"

Phil Zellis didn't move and didn't say anything. There probably was nothing he could say.

"Damn, none of you likes to talk, huh? Maybe we take you two hostage. What do you think about that, Mr. Beverly Hills?"

After a long moment of silence, I spoke. "That'd be a mistake," I said.

The guy looked over at me, took a final puff of his cigarette, and calmly threw it on the floor without stamping it out. "Who the hell are you again? You the friend, right?"

"Right."

"The friend that's about to get his brains splattered all over the floor," he said. "Hey, Ax. You feel like shooting this *pendejo*?"

Ax was apparently the guy with the gun at my temple. He started to laugh. "Maybe I will. Let's see him give me a good reason why I shouldn't pop him right now. Come on, *maricon*. What you got to say?"

"Shooting me is bad luck," I said, looking straight ahead.

"Just like taking us hostage would be."

"Oh, and why's that?"

"Because then there's no one left that has any cash. You take us hostage, there goes your money. There'll be no one around to pay you."

Ax jammed the gun closer to my head. "Oh, yeah? This rich guy here's got a wife, right? Bet you she'd pay big bucks to get him back."

"Bet you she won't. If you threaten to shoot him, she'll just say go ahead. That way she'll be the one to get all his money. And if you shoot either of us, then those Beverly Hills cops come back here. Just like they did the other day. Mister Alex Solis."

There was a short period of silence that hung over the room. I looked around the small guest house. It was one big, dirty room with an old refrigerator and a sink with streaks of rust on the far side. There were two doors, one that was probably a closet, the other a bathroom. Like the neighborhood, the whole place seemed as if it had seen better days.

"How'd you know my name?" he demanded.

"You rented the white van. You brought it over to Beverly Hills. The first time you went after Amanda. She was with her boyfriend at the time."

There was another moment of silence before Alex Solis got his bearings again. "You think you're a pretty smart dude, huh? So tell us. What's our next move, smart guy?"

"You can still get out of this," I lied. They really couldn't get out of this. Not with two dead bodies associated with them. These were easy collars for law enforcement, hoodlums who had been seen interacting, even in a tertiary way, with murder victims. With no one else handy, the police would squeeze them until they confessed. And even if they didn't confess, there was a good chance they'd be convicted in a trial. Depending on the location of the court, and getting a prosecutor who would throw enough circumstantial evidence at them, a jury was as likely to convict as not.

"Tell me how I do that? Tell me how I, ha ha, get out of this," he said with a fake laugh. I felt the gun move slightly away from my head.

"Look, you've done nothing wrong thus far. Couple of punches thrown, no big deal. Amanda looks like she's okay, she hasn't been harmed. Call it a misunderstanding. If we don't press charges, this all goes away. Just let us go."

"Let you go?" bellowed the guy who had been holding the cigarette. "The fuck we will. We got you here, and you're not going anywhere. And you'll do what we tell you to do. This bitch here owes the boss a ton of money and we're gonna get it. If not, maybe we just use you for target practice. Then we cut you up and feed you to our dogs. Let you go, huh? No way."

"Yeah, but the only way you get the money is if you let us go. No one's left to bring it to you. That's your only play. If you want to get paid, that is."

"Maybe we'll call that TV network she's on. They might pay to get her back."

"I can help you negotiate that. I know some people there. Let me be your go-between."

There was an awkward silence before he spoke again. "You think we're stupid? We ain't letting you go. We ain't doing shit," he said, but for a moment he was at a loss for what to say next. And I knew at that moment there was an opportunity, one that might not come again. If they took us and tied us up, we were at their mercy. I still had my gun, but I did not have a good way to get to it. And even if I did, there was no telling how many of them had guns. But for the moment, only Alex had his gun drawn. It was this moment when I needed to act, because there was a distinct possibility that this moment might not come again. If they tied us up, we were as good as dead.

Alex Solis was on my left, and Phil was on my right. There were five guys standing near Amanda. I swung my left arm quickly upward and grabbed Alex's right wrist. Twisting it sharply, I bent his wrist back until he released his grip on the gun. I grabbed the gun with my left hand, and with my right, I delivered two sharp punches to the nose. There are few better ways to stun someone than by punching them in the nose. I transferred the gun to my right hand, my shooting hand, and grabbed Alex by the hair with my left. Alex slid backward, but I kept him upright by yanking tightly on his hair. I moved behind him, using his body as a shield, and put the gun to his cheek, where everyone could see it.

"Anyone moves, Alex gets killed!" I yelled as loud as I could.

"Hey what the … ?" said one.

"Yo, you gonna get yourself shot, *puta*," said another.

"Amanda!" I screamed at her. "Get over here now!"

"Hey, bitch, you ain't going … "

"I said now! Get over here now, move … RIGHT NOW … or I'm blowing Alex's face all over this floor!"

Amanda hesitated but she was now in motion, moving toward us. I pushed the gun hard into Alex's face and let go of his hair for a moment. Reaching into my pocket with my left hand, I grabbed the Pathfinder keys and tossed them to Phil.

"Start it up now!" I shouted. "Take Amanda!"

The two of them raced out the door. I grabbed Alex's hair again. I saw one guy reach into his pocket. I pointed over his head and fired a shot that missed him by ten feet. But the shot was loud and the shot was an attention-getter. The guy stopped reaching for something. Everyone froze for a moment.

"I'm walking out of here now! You want to see Alex alive again, nobody follows us! You got it?!"

I didn't bother to wait for a response; instead, I jerked Alex toward the door and waved the gun menacingly. There was confusion and no one seemed to know quite what to do. Fortunately, I did. As I backed out of the guest house, I raised the gun and walloped Alex over the head. He collapsed in a heap. I threw the gun into the next-door neighbor's backyard and took off for the street on a dead sprint. Phil had started up the Pathfinder and was pulling out as I ran toward them. Behind me I heard some commotion and heard some cursing. The back door of the Pathfinder swung open, and I jumped in. Reaching around, I grabbed the handle and pulled the door shut. I saw the gang dash toward the street as we pulled away. Gunfire ripped through the air.

"Duck!" I yelled, lowering my head.

Both Phil and Amanda moved their heads forward, although Phil still needed to drive. I heard a rear tail light smash and the plunking sound of bullets hitting metal. Phil floored it, and we speeded out of the neighborhood. He made a couple of wild turns, as we wound our way back onto Rosecrans. He blew right through a red light, honking his horn at a startled motorist. We sped quickly down Rosecrans and were lucky to have a few lights turn green for us along the way. Phil pulled onto the northbound Largo Beach Freeway and gunned the engine. I watched traffic through the back window for the next mile. No one entered the freeway from that on-ramp and no one was following us.

"Are you okay?" I asked them.

"Scared out of my wits, but yes," Amanda said.

"I'm okay," Phil said, his breathing heavy. "But I could use a drink right about now. You?"

I took a deep breath and tried to relax.

"Not really," I finally said. "But we need to talk. And I don't think we should do it in Beverly Hills. Or Culver City."

"What do you suggest?"

I thought for a moment. "I haven't eaten since five-thirty this morning. You both like Mexican food? I know a good place on the way."

Eleven

El Tepeyac has been an institution since the 1950s, oddly situated on a residential street in Boyle Heights. This East L.A. neighborhood has been a Latino bastion for as long as I could remember, and probably for decades before that. But prior to World War II, this was actually a Jewish enclave. The main cross street was once called Brooklyn Avenue, ostensibly named to try and attract New Yorkers who had grown tired of the harsh winters. Brooklyn Avenue had been renamed Cesar Chavez Avenue, the Big Apple transplants and their offspring had long since scattered to other parts of L.A., and the desire to draw any more people from the East Coast was now quaint to even think about.

The restaurant was a frequent haunt of cops from the Hollenbeck station, especially back in the days when uniformed cops were allowed to take a Code 7 meal break. The Code 7 was eliminated years ago during union negotiations, but it was not uncommon to see cops swing by here after a shift. The place was famous for their large portions and especially for their burritos. The most infamous burrito at El Tepeyac was the Manuel's Special, named after the restaurant's founder. It was a massive, five-pound mound of a meal, roughly the size of a football, and designed to feed a family of four. It was essentially a pork burrito, stuffed with rice, beans and God knows what else, topped with cheese, more pork, and some type of spicy red sauce. They also had a special challenge that any one person who could finish a Manuel's Special by themselves in under one hour got a t-shirt and had their picture hung on the restaurant's wall of fame. I decided to live in obscurity and ordered the smaller, more manageable Hollenbeck burrito. Amanda and Phil went straight for the drinks menu.

We sat at a table inside of a brick-lined archway. The waitress quickly brought a basket of glistening tortilla chips just out of the fryer, and set a bowl of *salsa verde* down next to it. Amanda and Phil each asked for a double shot of tequila, and after quickly throwing those back, Amanda ordered a blended margarita. Phil told the waitress he wanted another double shot. I looked at them carefully before I asked Phil for my Pathfinder keys back. I took a sip from my Coke. I was glad I had ordered it with extra ice.

"We need to talk about what happened," I said to both of them, but looking straight at Amanda.

"I'm not ready to discuss it," she replied and took a long sip of margarita through a straw.

"Well, get ready. You're going to talk to me, or you're going to talk to the police. Or maybe both."

"Hey," she replied, "I've been through a lot here."

"I don't care. Whatever you've been through needs to be

talked about. Especially in a kidnapping plot where the supposed victim didn't appear to be bound or gagged."

Amanda looked down and said nothing. I continued.

"Let me run through all this. Tell me when I've gotten something wrong. Or maybe fill in some missing pieces. Your grandfather played poker each week. A couple of the guys he played with referee college football games?"

Amanda still looked down, but at least she nodded.

"So, somewhere along the line last year, these refs told your grandfather about shaving points off of games they were working. Maybe throwing a penalty flag at a key moment? Or negating a touchdown, saying the ball didn't cross the plane of the goal line? Maybe kicking a star player out of the game? Something to give the team they were betting on an edge? Make some money on the side?"

"No," she said, finally looking up, but her face was grim.

"No what?"

"No. They didn't tell Grandpa what they were doing. He told them what to do. He made them do it."

I leaned back and took another sip of Coke. "How did your grandfather do that?"

"These refs owed him some money. Grandpa had a lot of cash and he loaned it out. When they had trouble paying him back, he told them what they needed to do to get whole."

I took this in. "Okay. That clears up one area. But everything else still fits. These refs start making sure the right team covers the spread. Or doesn't cover the spread. Whatever. And Grandpa told them which team to help out. Then he let you in on things. So you could make some money. Maybe look like a big shot in his granddaughter's eyes."

"Yeah," she muttered. "Something like that."

I turned to Phil. "And were you part of this?"

Phil shook his head and glared at Amanda. "First I've heard of it. They didn't tell me. Sometimes grandparents want to have a special connection to their grandkids."

"Yeah, this was special all right," I said dryly and turned back to Amanda. "And in the beginning you were making a lot of money. The refs came through and the bets paid off. How much did you make?"

"I don't know."

"Wyatt was in on it, too, I gather."

She looked at me oddly. "He was making some bets. How did you know?"

"Lucky guess. But maybe he used some of his winnings to buy that white Jaguar?"

She gave a short laugh. Maybe more of a snort. "Yeah, maybe."

"Hey, Amanda got herself a brand new Mercedes, too," Phil said, starting to feel the effects of the tequila. "I just assumed she was doing well at her job. Goes to show what the hell I knew about this."

"I take it you weren't big on sharing your money with your kids," I said to Phil. "Let them find their own way."

Phil's eyes narrowed. "It worked for me."

"Oh, right. After your dad sent you to Vassar. You found your way into a Beverly Hills family with lots of money and a business that needed running. Nice work if you can get it. But after a while, you started skimming off the top. Setting yourself up for after the divorce from wife number one."

"Hey," Phil warned, re-engaged and wagging a finger indelicately at me. "Hey, watch your mouth."

"Or what? You're going to take a swing at me? Sorry, but I've already been shot at today, so I don't think your threats are going to scare me now."

"Still," he said, looking sheepish.

"And then you started losing money on the bets," I said, turning back to face Amanda. "So something must have happened."

"Yeah," she sighed. "The conference started to take a hard look at the games those refs were working. In one, OSU, the team we were betting on, was favored to win by 10 points and they were up 21-7, everything looked good. But then they fumbled the ball right at the end of the game, and Fresno's defense picked it up and ran it in for a touchdown. OSU would have still won, but it would have made the score 21-14, and we wouldn't have covered the spread. So the refs threw a penalty flag and called something, I don't know, illegal use of the hands on Fresno. It was totally bogus, but it wiped out the touchdown and OSU kept the score at 21-7. That's how it ended. We won our bet. Similar thing happened a week later, so the conference started an investigation."

"And those crooked refs didn't bother to tell you about that?"

"The refs learned right before kickoff of the next game. They found out their officiating was being monitored, so they couldn't do anything to help us. We lost a huge bundle. Grandpa ordered them to shave points off of a game the following week, but that didn't happen. I guess the refs didn't want to risk going to jail. All of a sudden, I'm down fifty thousand."

"Decided not to ask Grandpa for a loan?"

She shook her head no. "He lost a bundle, too."

"Okay. Then what happens next is you owe the bookies a pile of money you can't pay back. Is that the reason those thugs in the white van jumped you a few nights ago?"

"Yeah. They're the leg breakers. They try and smack you around as a warning. Pay up or else."

"And you nailed them with some pepper spray," I said.

Amanda stared at me. "Wouldn't you? I knew we owed them, and I'd told them they'd get their money. But they didn't think it was happening fast enough."

"Who's this Mike White?"

Amanda coughed. "I don't know, I've never met him. I guess he runs the outfit from a distance. He uses those guys in Compton to collect and to pay off. They get a percentage."

"All right. So you started trying to hit up men you knew who had some money. Pro football players always have money. Guys like Xavier Bishop and Rhett McCann. But they weren't thrilled about handing you tens of thousands of dollars just for a few tastes of the honey pot."

"Hey," broke in Phil, louder than was necessary. "Watch your mouth. I'm serious. This is my daughter you're talking to."

"Your daughter almost got us killed, Phil. Let's stick with the facts."

"Find another way to put it," he said.

I gawked at him. "Sure. I'll see if I can be more respectful to a girl who doesn't seem to have much respect for you or me. Or anyone or anything. Other than money, that is."

"Those players didn't give me any money," Amanda said, looking away.

"No, so you stole some. Rhett McCann told me about it. He wasn't going to press charges, because he doesn't need the money and didn't want to go through the public humiliation for being swindled. Or being slapped around by a girl with a pretty face. But there's something else here, probably more important."

"What's that?"

"Rhett McCann wasn't about to get roped into whatever illegal activities you're involved in. The NFL takes a dim view of players even associating with gamblers, much less ones involved in point-shaving. He'd rather walk away from ten thousand dollars than press charges and be caught up in a scandal."

Amanda took a deep breath. The waitress came by with my burrito and set it down next to me. Steam rose from it. Phil motioned to the waitress and ordered yet another round of tequila. If I were in his position, I'd have been tempted to order a bottle. All of this seemed new to him and none of it seemed good.

"So you got some money, Amanda, but it clearly wasn't enough. You owed fifty large. And your father here overreacted by putting Moose Machado in charge of protecting you. Sounds like he was the one who could have used the protecting. You're a lot more dangerous than he ever would be."

"What are you talking about?" Phil asked, starting to look a little bleary-eyed. "Moose was a monster."

"No, Phil," I said. "Moose was just big. And dumb. He

made some bad bets, and he was the one who introduced Amanda to the bookie. Amanda couldn't just go up to Vegas, where someone might have learned about her gambling and put two and two together. That would have gotten her fired in an instant. No, she got Moose to make the introduction to his bookie. And then when she got in over her head, she and those thugs in Compton cooked up a kidnapping scheme to get daddy to pay the ransom. Guess it came as a surprise to her when you turned down the request."

"How did that lead to Moose getting killed?" Phil asked.

"Moose was expendable," I said, looking hard at Amanda, who averted my gaze. "He was meant to be an example of what happened if you didn't cough up the ransom money. But you were right, Phil. Something about all of this really didn't smell good."

Phil stared at me. I continued.

"What got my antenna up was when I heard they were asking for five hundred grand," I said to Amanda. "You only owed fifty. You and those grease balls were planning to con your father and then split the rest."

Amanda's face tightened, and she said nothing.

"But I've seen these things go down before. Sometimes the crooks split the money fifty-fifty and sometimes they don't."

"Meaning?" she asked.

"You might have wound up in the same place as Moose. Figuratively speaking and all."

Amanda picked up her glass and bent over. She tugged hard on the straw. After a few seconds a slurping sound was emitted, and she stopped. I cut open a corner of my burrito and took a bite. It tasted pretty good, and it tasted just like it had when I first came here at age nineteen. The world changes, but thankfully a few things stay the same.

I swallowed and continued. "Tell me something. How did those guys know where Ed lived? You had to have given them the address, right?"

Her eyes flared. "No. No way. Grandpa was supposed to drop off the money on a side street near USC. Put it in a bag, drop it into a garbage can, and keep walking. But Grandpa didn't put any money in the bag, it was filled with blank paper. Really ticked those guys off. He tried to follow them back to Compton, but they caught on and lost him. Then they checked him out on the internet and went to his house. I don't think they meant to kill him, they were going to just threaten him, but they said things got out of hand."

I turned away in disgust. Ed Zellis could have called any one of a number of police departments. He could have paid the money. He could have not paid the money. But instead he chose to use his aging detective skills to try and capture some bad guys. He had lost his touch, if he ever had any to begin with, and it cost him his life.

I glared at Amanda. "And when you heard what happened, you just played along."

"I was in too deep. I couldn't just up and leave. We were trying to come up with another plan. It's tough to know the right thing to do."

"I'm sure you would have gotten to the right thing," I said. "After you exhausted all of the other possibilities. But let me tell you the only option you've got left."

"What's that?" she asked, gulping.

I looked at her and then down at my plate. Taking a big

bite of my burrito, I chewed it slowly. The pork was good, but next time I decided to try the chicken. Healthier and all.

"Two people are dead," I reminded her, "as a direct result of your actions. You may or may not have pulled the trigger, but they're dead nevertheless. If you hadn't have done what you did, Moose and Ed would be alive. You're complicit. If you start a fire, you don't get any credit for putting it out."

"Are you suggesting I'm guilty of murder?" she demanded. "That's outrageous. Me killing two people I was close to? That's absurd. No one would ever believe that."

"Maybe yes, maybe no. But you're an accessory, and I'll bet a case can be built that you were part of a conspiracy to commit murder. You could get sent away for life. True or not, here's how it'll play out. You'll be arrested and charged, along with the rest of that crew. The prosecutors will recognize your father has a lot of money and can buy the best lawyers. He may not do so, all things considered, but they'll be wary. Unless it's a high-profile case and they actually want a public spectacle, prosecutors don't always like a long, drawn-out legal battle. Their goal is to close cases. People like you are an annoyance, you don't always follow the script because you think your money will buy you freedom. The reality is it will only buy you some extra time."

Amanda stared at me. "Just what are you saying?"

"I'm saying there's a good chance you'll have the opportunity to turn state's evidence in exchange for a lighter sentence. You'll have to work with the police and identify the guys who did pull the triggers. You may even have to testify against them in open court. And for that, you'll get significantly less jail time. Maybe even none."

"I'm not going to be a rat," she said.

I rolled my eyes. "You've watched too many mob shows. You may think you're being a rat, but you're not. You're aiding law enforcement. This is how the game is played."

"You're pretty sure of yourself," she managed. "You don't know that all this can be proven. And good luck trying to convince people I had anything to do with getting my grandpa murdered. That's ridiculous."

"No, it's not. Maybe you didn't intend for that to happen, but it won't matter. Someone who gets into a fistfight may just want to give the other guy a fat lip. But if the other guy hits his head on the ground and dies after being punched, it suddenly becomes a homicide. Best laid plans and all."

She stared at me. "Well, that's not fair."

"The world isn't always about being fair. But it's just. And as to being able to prove this, remember, if I can unravel this, the police can, too. I just do it a little faster, is all. And trust me, there will be proof. They will have access to identify every phone call you made and everywhere you drove. There is no privacy any more. Everyone's life is an open book these days."

"That stinks," she said and sunk down into her chair.

"Oh, I don't know. I think it makes for a more honest society," I said, and focused on my burrito, working to spear more pork and less tortilla. I used the knife to maneuver some rice and beans and what might have been guacamole onto my fork. I shoveled it into my mouth and once again marveled at the flavor. I finally turned back to Amanda. "Don't you think that's true?"

"I don't know what to think any more. Look, I just saw a

way to make some money. Making money's the American way, isn't it? I didn't shoot anyone. I didn't hurt anyone. I'm a victim here."

I sighed. The burrito was hitting the spot; waffles at five-thirty in the morning can only take you so far into the day. The waitress came by with Phil's next shot of tequila. He tossed it down and smacked the shot glass on the table a little harder than he should have.

"Let me ask you something," Phil bellowed, his voice starting to slur. "What about that punk, that Wyatt. That Wyatt Angstrom."

I looked over at Amanda, who shrugged and looked away. "He's nothing," she said.

"Nothing?" Phil asked.

"He wasn't involved in all this. He was just a guy helping me in my career. He gave me what I wanted, I gave him what he wanted."

Phil and I both gaped at her for a long minute, not needing to ask for more details. At that point, my phone buzzed. I looked down and saw that it was an LAPD headquarters number. I wasn't sure who it was from, but I decided to take it. If you don't feel like answering the phone when the LAPD calls, there is a chance they may show up on your doorstep when they feel like it, usually at an ungodly hour.

"Hello."

"Burnside, it's Juan."

"My old pal. We just saw each other this morning. Say, did you change your mind? Put in a good word and ask the chief for a meeting?"

There was a long pause on the other end. "No. I did not. But funny things happen in life, you know?"

"Such as?" I asked.

"The chief. He just stopped by my office. He wants to see you. I don't know why and I don't know what for. But he wants to see you. Like now. How fast can you get your butt over here?"

*

I briefly thought of making a citizen's arrest of Amanda Zeal. But that was complicated, and having her woozy father nearby did not help matters. The difficulty in making a citizen's arrest is that detaining a culprit opens the citizen himself up to a host of potential criminal charges, including false imprisonment and kidnapping. And while I could justify that I had reasonable cause for suspecting Amanda Zeal was involved in a conspiracy to commit blackmail, fraud, and murder, my evidence was little more than a trail of breadcrumbs that I mixed together into a shaky pile. I was confident I was right, but I was not confident it could be proven. And even after our conversation at El Tepeyac, the only person witnessing her response was her father, who had just lost his own father to gun violence, and who was well on his way toward getting himself seriously inebriated.

As I drove over to LAPD headquarters, I admonished Amanda not to do anything rash and not to leave the car. I would be away for maybe half an hour. I told her that since she was a TV personality and well known, there was no place for her to run to, no way she could hide. Her best move, really, her only move would be to stay in the car and let me try and make arrangements. Phil groggily agreed to get her a lawyer, and I told her she had the opportunity to get out of this with a minimum of damage. If she ran, however, she'd be looking at spending the better part of her life in federal lockup. I didn't get her to verbally agree, but I did think some of my admonition sunk in. When I asked her and Phil for their phones, they handed them over without an argument. I walked to the back of my Pathfinder and surreptitiously stowed my weapon. Neither Phil nor Amanda seemed to notice.

After taking the elevator up to Chief Bates' office, I waited for fifteen minutes to see him. His assistant was disarmingly pretty, a well-proportioned girl wearing a business suit. But there was a lump under her arm, and I saw the slight hint of a handgun. I guess if you work for the chief, you'd better be fully invested in law enforcement.

The door to the chief's office swung open, and out walked Pete Bates, looking a little thicker than I'd remembered. The chief was solidly built, with a mass of salt-and-pepper hair, and small, dark eyes that felt like they could bore a hole right through you. He still kept his bushy cop mustache, a nice touch from bygone days when nearly every cop on every beat seemed to have one. He did not wear a uniform; instead, he had on a dark gray suit, blue button-down shirt, and a pink tie. He looked more like an executive than a cop. Appropriate, yet I still remembered him when he was a detective in the North Hollywood Division. He had come a long way.

"The famous Mr. Burnside," he declared, shaking my hand

and leading me into his plush office with soft carpeting and comfy-looking chairs. Once inside, he closed the door and pointed to a seat facing his desk. He made a spectacle of slowly walking around his desk and taking a deep sigh before sitting down and staring directly at me for a good ten seconds without saying a thing. I finally broke the silence.

"I never knew you to be at a loss for words, Pete," I finally managed. "Unless you're just trying to intimidate me. Or set up a dramatic moment, after which I fall on the floor crying."

Pete Bates gave me an exasperated look. "Still with the smart remarks. And you can call me chief, not Pete."

"Sure. But I'm just trying to get the conversation going," I said. "I don't think a busy guy like you would bring me in just to have a staring contest."

"No, I didn't bring you up here for that. And I am a busy guy, and I don't have time to waste."

"Good. Me neither. What's up?"

"What's up?" he exclaimed. "Suppose you tell me. I walk in this morning and learn my friend Ed Zellis has been shot to death in his own house. The chief at Culver called me, he knew Ed and I were poker buddies. I asked for some background and your name came up. I'm hearing your name a lot lately."

"I do get around," I shrugged.

"More than you should. Last I saw you, you were working vice out of North Hollywood. Over a decade ago. That was around the beginning of the end of your checkered career."

"I remember."

"Uh-huh. Reputations are earned and you've got one. Tell me what else you remember. How about explaining why I got a call from the county sheriff this afternoon. It seems like you were involved in a shooting in Compton."

"Mostly getting shot at," I pointed out.

"Mostly?!"

"Look, it's a little complicated," I started.

"Well unpack it for me. None of this is in my jurisdiction, but since I know Ed, I've got an interest here."

"Well, it started a few decades ago. Ed was a dirty cop down in Largo Beach PD."

Chief Bates glared at me. "Dirty cop? No, he wasn't. Not at all. Ed was a good man."

"Maybe the Ed you knew. The other Ed made a living out of ripping off drug dealers. You ever wonder why an ex-cop was living in such a great house up on Culver Crest?"

Pete Bates looked down at his mahogany desk and continued to shake his head in disgust. "Ed told me he made a fortune betting on tech stocks when the internet got red hot. I don't see why it's that hard to believe. And I'm a little tired of hearing about corruption every time a cop has some financial success outside of his work. This is America, after all."

"Land of opportunity," I agreed. "But be that as it may, Ed found a new hobby in retirement. Betting on football games."

"Well, there's something you never hear of. People betting on sports. Yeah, I know it's not legal, not yet anyway. But I'm not going to worry about minutia like that when I have robberies and homicide cases on my watch that I need to clear."

"He wasn't just betting on games. He was fixing them."

Pete Bates froze, and he stared at me for a long moment.

It did not seem staged, and it did not seem to be a tactic. He seemed genuinely at a loss for words. I continued.

"You played poker with Ed and a bunch of guys. Some ex-cops, some ex-football players. A few referees, too. Something else you probably didn't know was that Ed had another side hustle going on. He was a shylock. He was lending money to the refs. When they couldn't make their vig, he coerced them into shaving points on football games."

I watched Chief Bates carefully. The tactics Ed Zellis had employed came right out of organized crime's handbook. It was a mob strategy. Once they got their meat hooks into someone, they would fleece them any way they could. In Ed's case, I didn't know why he went down this route; Ed didn't seem to need the money. Maybe he needed people to fear him. That's why some guys become cops. And why some guys then become ex-cops.

"So, that's what got him killed?" Chief Bates managed.

"It led to a string of events, but yes. Ed began winning money when the teams he bet on won. The games the refs fixed. He told his granddaughter about it, and she told her boyfriend. Maybe someone else, a family acquaintance, and he didn't meet a good ending, either. The granddaughter's name is Amanda Zeal, you might have seen her on TV a few times. Near as I can tell, the secret didn't get any farther. But then some conference officials began getting suspicious. The refs apparently called some penalties that were just patently absurd. So an investigation began."

"Did Ed get caught up in it?"

"No, but the refs stopped helping. And then Ed started losing. But Amanda began losing in much larger chunks. She owed a lot of money to some bad people. They went after her, and they went hard. Attacked her in front of her apartment building. That's where I came in. Ed's son Phil hired me to look into what was going on with her."

"Go on."

"You probably heard about that homicide in Beverly Hills this week. Anthony Machado. He was caught up in it, placed some bad bets and ended up a victim. That's when the granddaughter disappeared. Apparently she agreed to conspire with this gang to pretend she was kidnapped."

"Sounds like a lovely gal," he muttered.

"Yeah, I've seen better. They asked Amanda's father for five hundred grand. He turned them down."

"I don't know Ed's son very well. Does Phil even have five hundred grand to spare?" Chief Bates asked.

I rubbed my lower lip. "Yes. I'm sure he could find it if he wanted to. But Phil decided to call their bluff. Said no. Didn't want to give in to blackmailers."

Chief Bates nodded. "That I get. But I take it he didn't call in the FBI. Or anyone else in law enforcement. He was scared they would kill her if he did?"

"That's right. So after Phil said no, their next stop was Ed. He responded by falsely agreeing to pay the money, but instead tried to trick them into coming out into the open. At the drop, he left what was effectively an empty bag. When they took it, he followed them. At some point they had a face-to-face. That was yesterday. And this morning, Ed's body was found. Can't be certain if he was killed in his house, or somewhere else and the body was moved. My guess was at the house. Crooks aren't big on making deliveries. If they wanted to dump a body they probably would have just tossed him behind a Burger King somewhere."

"And you found out where someone in this gang lived. I take it that was Compton."

"It was. Phil and I went over there today. Mostly to see if we could find Amanda. Which we did. Mind if I ask you a question?"

Chief Bates threw up his hands. "Well, why not? I'm always happy to serve our P.I.s. Especially the ones involved in murder and mayhem."

"How did the sheriff's department know I was in Compton? I know all about license plate readers, but they're not on every intersection. And you normally don't get the results this fast."

"The incident was called in by one of the neighbors. They saw an altercation between some kids and a couple of old men."

"Old men?" I said, raising my eyebrows.

"They said the old men were beating up some kids. Then one of the kids pulled a gun and that stopped the fracas."

I processed this and wondered why the nosy neighbor didn't bother to call the cops right away, not because of a public brawl, but because two people were taken away at gunpoint. Instead they waited until we burst out of the house and roared off, a hail of bullets following us in our tracks. And the neighbor wrote down my license plate, somehow thinking Phil and I were at fault.

"The fracas stopped," I told him, "because we had a gun drawn on us. And then we managed to escape. So one of the good citizens of Compton calls the sheriff and reports me for getting shot at. Am I missing something here?"

"Look, I don't begin to put myself in the shoes of the citizenry. They saw something, they called it in. Better that they did than they didn't. But what were you two doing, going to Compton by yourselves?"

"Time was of the essence. We originally thought Amanda had been kidnapped, we needed to get her back, and we didn't have the ability to coordinate between a bunch of different police departments. I actually asked Juan if he could do that, but he turned me down."

"As well he should have," Bates said. "Two murders in two other cities and a girl being held hostage in a third. I can't say as I like it, but it's not up to the LAPD to lead the charge here."

"So yeah, I could have filled out an application with the county sheriff to investigate what turned out to be a false kidnapping orchestrated by a girl who'd had an affair with one of the deceased and who was the granddaughter of the other. Let that sink in. I'd have gotten more cooperation from TMZ."

"And then you two go off to Compton, find where Amanda is, get into a fistfight with a couple of gangbangers, have a gun pulled on you, and then escape with your lives. And now you're here. Do I have that timetable right?"

"Actually, we stopped for lunch first."

Chief Bates slapped his hand on his desk and looked up at the ceiling. He was probably wishing the weekend was here already. I was, too.

"All right," he continued. "In Compton, we now have a group of people who very likely had an involvement in two homicides, and they are walking around scot free. That is, if they haven't bolted for Mexico already. And Amanda Zeal could be on a plane to someplace in the world. Maybe one where they don't allow extradition."

"No," I said.

"No? What do you mean, no? Where is she?"

"She and Phil are waiting for me downstairs. They're in my car."

Bates stared at me. "Waiting downstairs? After all that's happened? How do you know they haven't disappeared into the wind?"

"Because I asked them not to."

"Oh, good heavens," Chief Bates said as he pushed a button on his intercom. A female voice came on the line. "Anderson. Get my detail. We're going out of the building."

"Yes, sir."

With that, Chief Pete Bates stood up and picked up a pair of sunglasses. He walked briskly around his desk and toward the door. Although he didn't actually invite me, I followed behind him. We walked down the hall to the elevator, where we were met by three middle-aged men wearing dark suits. The chief turned to me.

"What kind of a car do you have?" he asked.

"A black Pathfinder."

"Are either of these two armed?"

"Not to my knowledge."

The chief gave me another long stare. "Not to your knowledge. Well, let's hope they aren't. And let's hope they're still there. I may need to issue a citywide manhunt if they're not. There is nothing worse than a man whose child is in danger, I don't care how old the child is. The parents do dumb things and they're often reckless. And I can assure you, if anything happens as a result of their actions – in my jurisdiction – I swear, I'll have your license pulled."

I didn't say anything, and I didn't bother to inform the chief that my private investigator's license was issued by the state, not the city, and even if it were issued by the city, he didn't have the ability to pull it. But I decided it would be prudent to hold that comment for a bit. One step at a time. The elevator came, and as we rode down, the chief gave instructions to his detail. I would walk toward the car, his detail would be following me, a few paces back. If there were any indications of danger, don't hesitate to take someone out quickly. We were in a downtown area that was already in rush hour mode. Don't endanger innocent lives, even if it means overreacting to the suspects.

We walked out of the LAPD headquarters building and into the late afternoon. The tall buildings of downtown shielded us from direct sunlight. Shadows were forming, but it was still warm. I walked down the street to my Pathfinder, not entirely sure of what to expect. I absently brushed my right hand across my holster, but I remembered I had surreptitiously stowed my .357 away in the Pathfinder. I started getting nervous as we turned the corner. But as we approached my vehicle, my apprehension stopped. I rapped on the window, the gold wedding band on my ring finger doing all the damage that needed to be done, which is to say, make some loud noises. In an instant, and with little fanfare, I managed to jolt both Phil Zellis and Amanda Zeal awake from what appeared to be a very deep sleep. They blinked a few times and looked confused. I told them to get out of the vehicle. Real slow.

Twelve

On Monday morning, Amanda Zeal and six gang members were hauled into court and arraigned on multiple counts. Amanda was charged with conspiracy, fraud, and being an accessory to murder. Her lawyer was Preston J. Pierpont, a renowned criminal defense attorney who was best known for charging an arm and a leg, or in this case, a quarter of a million dollars for a retainer. It is likely Phil Zellis picked up the tab. Because of her public profile as what was generously referred to as a sports journalist, Amanda was the only one who had in-depth articles written about her in the *L.A. Times*. Not surprisingly, perhaps, she turned out to be the only one of the accused who was able to post bail, which escalated well into six figures.

Gail also had her name in the *Times* a few days later, when she publicly criticized City Attorney Jay Sutker of poor leadership, and of failing to exercise proper executive authority over his office. She also declared that the next mayor of Los Angeles should come from the city council, as they had both the breadth of experience and the keen wisdom to fulfill the duties of the office. Sutker responded quickly, endorsing Shane Karp for City Attorney and accusing Gail of politicizing her position. Shane Karp enthusiastically accepted Sutker's endorsement, calling him a great visionary.

Later that week, the *Times* ran an *exposé* of Jay Sutker, pointing to a variety of unsavory activities that began with questionable decision-making on deeming who to prosecute and ended with alleged abuse of power. Sutker immediately denounced the article as a hatchet job, but the next day, an op-ed piece appeared in the paper, written by a Korean businessman who owned a string of convenience stores. He accused Sutker of routinely refusing to prosecute shoplifters, and ignoring his pleas for justice. Finally, a woman in the public defender's office came forward with allegations of sexual misconduct, and that was that. Gail and I watched Sutker's press conference where he dropped out of the race, and resigned his position as City Attorney. Shane Karp was noticeably silent, and I didn't bother to mention the lurid photos I had found on his Facebook page; I doubted we would need them. But I did imagine that somewhere, Arthur Woo was enjoying the images of a disgraced rival, and that he had a cat-who-ate-the-canary smile on his face.

The Rams won their playoff game and advanced to the Super Bowl to play the Patriots. In the past few years, the Super Bowl was important to Marcus, mostly because of the wide variety of snacks we laid out. From mini hot dogs to barbecued potato chips, Super Bowl Sunday was second only to Halloween in being able to indulge in treats. We usually tried to have him eat healthy, but when I'm eating a stuffed-crust, meat-lovers pizza, it's difficult to say no to virtually any other culinary request.

This Super Bowl was particularly special because we got to host an honored guest. It is not every day that a pro football player accepts an invitation to come to your home, but when Xavier Bishop said yes, Marcus was especially thrilled. I had to admit, I was a little impressed, too.

In California, the opening kickoff for the Super Bowl is at three-thirty in the afternoon, so Marcus and I had some time to throw a Nerf football around in the backyard before I ran out to a crowded supermarket for more chips, and a few last minute ingredients to add to my guacamole recipe. Xavier arrived at a little after three, with a very pretty Desiree on one arm and a wicker basket on the other.

"Got a surprise for you!" he exclaimed.

"You brought Desiree," I said, introducing them to Gail and Marcus. "That is a very nice surprise."

"Not only that," he said. "She made my mama's special fried chicken recipe. You are going to love it."

"What's special about it?" asked Marcus.

"It's the crust. You like Cap'n Crunch cereal, young man? Well, this one's dipped in ground up Cap'n Crunch. Sweetest fried chicken crust you'll ever taste."

"Oh, wow!" Marcus yelled.

By comparison, my guacamole and chips paled when held up to the fried chicken. It was very good fried chicken. To Marcus, it was indeed the best thing in the world. Marcus managed to secure a drumstick before we were able to even put it on the table, and he bit into it with a smile on his face.

When Xavier sat down on the couch, Marcus asked him for an autograph, but X did him one better.

"Come here, little Burnside," he said and patted his lap. "We're doing a selfie together. You and me."

Marcus jumped into his lap, and I was thankful Xavier didn't have a drink in his hand at the time. He lifted Marcus up with one hand, a feat that was easily done when you bench press over three hundred pounds a day. With his other hand he snapped the picture and then air dropped it to my phone. I went and printed out a copy and gave it to Marcus. True to form, Marcus took it and went back to Xavier again to ask him to autograph it for him. This time Xavier laughed and agreed.

Desiree was helping Gail in the kitchen, and Marcus ran in to show her the autograph. Xavier turned to me with a smile on his face, albeit a wistful one.

"You got a great kid, there," he said.

"I know. We are blessed in more ways than I can count."

"How do you do it?" he asked.

I looked at him carefully. "What do you mean?"

"Desiree is due in May. I'm nervous already. So many things can go wrong with kids. I shouldn't be worried, but I'm worried. I've seen bad things happen to good kids. Too many times. How do I shake this fear? In everything else in life, I'm fearless. Not afraid of anything. I'll take on anyone, anywhere. But this? It's got me sidetracked."

"I hear you. But I've got to tell you that the feeling you described doesn't go away real easily. You want the best for your kids, but you know there'll be instances you can't protect them. You won't be around all the time. You just have to raise them right, teach them to defend themselves, tell them to treat people the way they want to be treated. And then hope the world takes good care of them. It usually does, although you never know. But the fear? It's like having butterflies before a big game. Doesn't ever fully go away. You just try and get the butterflies to fly in formation. You learn to live with it."

"Man, I never knew what being a parent would really be like. I always figured I'd get there, but I never thought through the details."

"It isn't as tough as you think. If you got this far, there's a good chance your kid will, too. Maybe even do better than you. Your kids will have advantages you didn't have."

"I hope so."

"How are you and Desiree getting on?" I asked.

"Good, real good. You know, she's so smart. I never really appreciated that in her until we started getting serious. She began law school this year. How about that? Me, married to a lawyer! Guess you and I are going to have something in common."

"Yeah," I said. "It's good to be partnered with someone smart. Beats the alternative."

"Ha! You know, Desiree told me she read something about Gail in the paper. That she might be running for City Attorney or something?"

"Looking pretty likely," I said. "Talk about worrying. If Gail ends up with a very public position, it means I'm going to be a public figure, too."

"Yeah, you already are. Former football player, former coach. Plus, once in a while I see your name in the papers.

Cracking some case."

"I try to keep a low profile. The private investigator title does have the word private in it."

"Speaking of which, I saw Amanda Zeal got busted this week. She's not going to look real hot in an orange jump suit. You have anything to do with that?"

I held my thumb and index finger close together. "Maybe a little."

"Yeah, uh-huh. Maybe a lot. I wonder if that means our friend Rhett McCann can stop worrying about Amanda."

"I don't think he has much to worry about on that score. Except he won't get back the ten grand Amanda stole from him."

"Ten grand?" Xavier said incredulously. "Damn. That girl was just plain trouble. Capital T. Well, Rhett'll be okay. You know the players on the winning team today walk away with two hundred thousand. Even the losing teams, the players get over fifty large. Just being on the roster of a Super Bowl team gives you a good payday."

"Nice work if you can get it," I smiled.

Gail and Desiree laid out the food on the table, I went and pulled a couple of Blue Moons from the refrigerator for Xavier and myself, and I got Marcus a Coke. Gail passed on a beer and Desiree rubbed her belly at the suggestion of something to drink, and said water would be just fine. We settled in and watched the game, which was mostly a defensive struggle. For Xavier and myself, it was a masterpiece; to everyone else, it was not. Marcus got bored in the second quarter and went off to his room to draw in a coloring book. Gail and Desiree chatted about law school.

Xavier and I gossiped about players we knew in the league, and how much time Johnny Cleary would have to get the Bears into the playoffs. I asked if Cliff Roper was still his agent, and he laughed and said yes. Cliff was still annoying, but he could deliver money to his clients like no one else. In the end, that's all that mattered in an agent.

We tried to think of some offensive plays that would work against two tough defenses. None sprung to mind. The Patriots were leading 7-6 near the middle of the fourth quarter. Rhett McCann was doing his job of clogging up the middle of the defensive line, preventing the Patriots from running effectively. But then the Patriots began to throw the ball successfully, and within three plays they had moved the length of the field. They were inside the Rams' 20 yard line. And then Rhett McCann stepped up his game.

The Patriots' quarterback dropped back into the pocket to fling another pass. But he never got the throw off. Rhett McCann blew past his blocker using a swim move, employing it to perfection. The swim move is a technique used by defensive linemen, and it is very similar to a freestyle swimming stroke. In this case, Rhett McCann started by quickly swinging his right arm and then his left arm directly over the helmet of the offensive lineman who was trying to block him. The lineman was distracted momentarily and backed up a step as Rhett surged forward. Rhett then used his right arm as leverage, this time swinging it across the lineman's right shoulder and pushing the lineman off balance. The lineman was immobilized briefly. Rhett then barreled past his blocker by swinging his left arm forward. The blocker hopped to his right and tripped. Rhett crashed into the quarterback before he could release the ball and, continuing to use his swim move, chopped the football out of the quarterback's grip. A Ram linebacker picked it up and raced fifty yards in the other direction before being tackled, ending up deep in Patriots' territory. It was now the Rams' ball and the Rams suddenly had control of the game.

"Wow!" exclaimed Xavier. "Did you see Rhett do that strip sack? That was perfection, man. Absolute perfection. That guy knows what he's doing."

I nodded in agreement. I reflected back on the past few weeks and wished that more people had known what they were doing. There's an old saying that life is tough, but it's tougher if you're stupid. Things ended up swimmingly for me. But things could have ended far better for others. And then some.

The End

About The Author

David Chill is a USA TODAY bestselling author. In addition to *Swim Move,* he has written ten other mystery novels as part of the Burnside Series: *Post Pattern, Fade Route, Bubble Screen, Safety Valve, Corner Blitz, Nickel Package, Double Pass, Tampa Two, Flea Flicker,* and *Hard Count.* David Chill's first novel, *Post Pattern,* was an award winner in the St. Martin's Press contest for First Private Eye Mystery Writers. He has also written a political thriller, *Curse Of The Afflicted.*

Born and raised in New York City, David Chill was educated in the public schools. After receiving his undergraduate degree from SUNY-Oswego, he moved to Los Angeles where he earned a Master's degree from the University of Southern California.

David Chill currently lives in Los Angeles with his wife and son. If you would like to contact David Chill directly, please email him at the following: davidchill3214@gmail.com

If you enjoyed Swim Move, then be sure to read the next great novel in David Chill's Burnside series....

Hard Count

Here is a sample chapter of this terrific mystery...

HARD COUNT PREVIEW

The truth about people often surprises us. But when you work with some of life's sketchier characters, as I often do, the truth normally does not come as a surprise at all.

Harold Stevens was an insurance fraud investigator I had known for many years. He had helped me through some rough patches in my life, not necessarily in the way some people do, by graciously listening to my troubles. Rather, Harold's input was mostly financial, steering business my way. And while money may be the root of certain types of evil, it can also be the tree that keeps you dry in an unyielding downpour. So, when Harold called and asked to get together, I happily agreed and suggested he pick the restaurant. I told him it would be my treat.

We were eating breakfast downtown at the Pacific Dining Car, which is ordinarily not the type of place I'd suggest for breakfast. The food was good, the service impeccable, and the décor, reminiscent of a 19th century railroad car, came complete with white linen tablecloths, and striped curtains to shield the glare of mid-morning sunlight. The restaurant was far more luxurious than most, a throwback to posh times, with a menu that offered everything from buttermilk biscuits to crab Benedict. Oddly, it was one of those rare upscale restaurants that remained open for 24 hours each day. Most McDonald's outlets didn't even bother with doing that anymore. But the Pacific Dining Car had been around for over a century and it was still a gourmet's delight, which naturally came part and parcel with gourmet-level prices. That it was still around, and still bustling was a little surprising. Restaurants in L.A. come and go, and even those longstanding, old-school places eventually had to shutter, often when their aging clientele began to both literally and figuratively die off.

We sat at a booth, with stately, pillow-enhanced wooden dividers rising high to preserve a modicum of privacy. Harold took a short sip of cream-laden coffee and gave a satisfied nod. He was a portly man, a little older than me, meaning we were both middle-aged, but he was showing it more than I was. Harold was bald, save for that small ring of dyed-black hair along the sides. It didn't look bad on him, but the male-pattern baldness did reflect his age, and in much of the world, that would not be unusual. In Los Angeles, however, anything that didn't scream youth and vibrancy was looked upon with a measure of distrust.

"So, thanks for calling me," I said. "I always get a good feeling when I see the Differential Insurance Company pop up on my phone."

"And I'm glad you were available," he answered. "I was wondering what your schedule was like. Gail's campaign is going into the home stretch. Primary day is a couple weeks away. You must be busy."

I took a sip of my black coffee. It was good, smooth coffee, but it lacked the punch of my over-caffeinated Starbucks French roast.

"I see you're following the campaign. But yes, I'm spending more time with Marcus," I said. My wife, Gail Pepper, was embarking on a political career, running for City Attorney of Los Angeles. Public life was new terrain for her, but not for me. She was entering politics for the first time, and I was re-entering life in the public eye once more. As a former college football coach, I was used to managing the spotlight, even if my unseemly past got dredged up once in a while. But as a newly minted political spouse, I had to take great pains to avoid saying the wrong thing to a reporter, and had to pull a few punches in more ways than one. In some instances, I failed miserably.

"How's the race looking?" he asked. "I hear Arthur Woo is a shoo-in for mayor. That should be good for Gail. He endorsed her."

"It helped. But the last poll I saw was a few weeks ago. She was ahead, but it was still a close race. We hadn't anticipated Paul Bleeker would jump in at the last minute. I guess he saw an opportunity. Or maybe he's using this to promote his law practice."

"Is Bleeker formidable?"

"He's rich," I replied, thinking the erstwhile lawyer had the brainpower equivalent to that of a maple tree. "So, yes. That makes him formidable."

"Do you have a role in the campaign?"

"Yeah. Staying out of the way."

Harold smiled. "Well, I have something that should keep you busy for a little bit."

"Love to hear it."

"You remember Curtis Starr? First-round draft pick, used to play middle linebacker for the Rams years ago. Among other teams."

I nodded. Nearly everyone knew about Curtis, but maybe not for football, or even for his short-lived film career. Hollywood thought he had leading-man looks, so they cast him in a few movies, only to discover he had limited talent as an actor. He found his calling in food, however, investing in a restaurant, that quickly evolved into a successful chain. It was likely people knew him more for his brisket and ribs than for anything else. And as the restaurants grew, so did his waistline, and his acting career became a thing of the past.

"Sure," I said. "Curtis was a few years before my time. Came out of a small school, if I remember."

"You recall right. Went to Middle Tennessee State of all places. Funny how many NFL players went to small colleges."

I sipped some more coffee. I knew from my coaching days at USC that there was some amazing high school football talent that went surprisingly unnoticed, and did not get recruited by the big-name colleges. Some of these kids had the misfortune of playing behind a star in high school. Others were late bloomers. A few of these kids got lucky the way Curtis Starr got lucky. He received a scholarship offer from a college scout who was at one of his games to recruit a player from an opposing team.

"So, it's been a few decades since he played pro football," I said. "He was one of those players who could go from pushing around smaller guys at Western Kentucky to going up against the studs on the Cowboys and 49ers."

"Curtis did all right for himself. Financially, too. Signed a big rookie contract, got a lot of guaranteed money. Invested it well, he owns that Smoky Mountain Grill chain. Among other things."

"And," I added, "I believe he has a son who's a football player, too. Used to be quarterback at Roche High. Not too far from here, in fact. Right next to downtown."

Harold slapped the table. "I knew I had the right investigator for this job. You know Brady?"

"Sure. We tried to recruit him when I coached at SC. Big arm, but he had a bit of an attitude problem. And a more important problem was his grades were atrocious. Seriously, I doubt he ever cracked a book in high school. We literally couldn't get him admitted. Believe it or not, there are still a few academic standards for football players to get accepted into a good college. Wound up at San Diego State. Less prominent school, just like his dad. Maybe for different reasons, though. Is Brady in some kind of trouble?"

"I don't think so. I'm more concerned about his father. I've known him for a long time. It seems the police have paid a few visits to his house. Domestic disputes, neighbors hearing arguments. Two nights ago there was some gunfire. The police investigated, but couldn't find out anything."

"What happened?"

"The neighbors heard a few gunshots. I suppose it could have been a car backfiring."

"Possible, but unlikely," I said. Modern vehicles just don't backfire much.

"I know," Harold agreed. "And they live up in Mandeville Canyon. I think you also know the chances of that happening around midnight. In that neck of the woods. Might have been fireworks."

"True," I said. Mandeville Canyon was an exclusive neighborhood in the hills above Brentwood, and while a few tourists and work crews might drive around there during the day, it was mostly local residents at night. "And so you think something else happened."

"I'm a seasoned investigator," Harold smiled. "But there's only so much I can do from the insurance company's standpoint. This is where you come in."

"Ah. I knew there was a reason for this breakfast," I said, noticing a white-suited waiter approaching us with a tray held high over his head. He set it down on a rack and picked up one of the plates.

"Now, who is the eggs Benedict?" he asked.

"That would be me," Harold said.

"And you must be the roast beef hash," the waiter declared, placing a white plate in front of me. It was piled with chopped prime rib and diced potatoes, and crowned with a poached egg. The waiter told us to enjoy, and quickly departed.

I cut the egg and let some orange yolk ooze slowly over the hash. "It's interesting this place stays open 24 hours," I said. "Just like Denny's. But the clientele is a wee bit different."

"Indeed," he said as he took a bite. I did the same, and savored my dish. It was good roast beef hash, but it was still hash, and I doubted even having prime rib as an ingredient could justify the price. But, if you could afford to pay twenty-two dollars for an order of hash, this was the place to get it. We each savored a few bites in silence. Then Harold spoke.

"So, let me tell you about this assignment," Harold said.

"Please."

"The back story is that Curtis took out a large life insurance policy a couple of years ago when he remarried. Ten million. Another one for his new wife, also ten million. We normally don't insure for such a high amount, but, well, he's a long-term client and he owns a very successful business. And he's attached to the business. His name is on the sign, and when you walk into any of his restaurants the first thing you see are photos of him."

"And without Curtis, there's maybe not much of a business."

"The business revolves around his image, he's in every commercial. Take away Curtis, you're selling the same chicken and ribs anyone else sells, only more expensive. Curtis decided he needed to take care of his family if anything happened to him. High premiums, but he could afford them."

"And just what is it you'd like from me?"

Harold brushed his lips lightly with a white cloth napkin. "As I mentioned, the policies are for ten million."

"And the Differential Insurance Company would like to avoid paying out ten million."

"That would be nice."

"You want me to find out what happened the other night," I mused.

"It would be to our benefit to have things simmer down," Harold said. "And to the benefit of everyone involved. I'd like you to look out for him."

"Sure. But tell me something. Unless he fails to pay the premium, you can't up and cancel a life insurance policy, can you? Just because his life is suddenly in danger?"

"Typically, no. But as I mentioned, this is not a standard policy. With a large payout comes a large level of added risk. There are special clauses included, one of which is the insured can't engage in dangerous activities. Like, say, skydiving or driving a race car."

"Or engaging in gunplay?" I asked, taking a forkful of hash and making sure it was draped with a sufficient amount of egg yolk.

"Perhaps. But we're getting into a gray area here."

I thought about this. When I was with the LAPD, we were once called about a man who was walking his dog on his neighbor's lawn. The dog got into a scuffle with the neighbor's dog, and in trying to break up the fight, the man had a heart attack and died. I heard later that the man's life insurance company refused to pay on the grounds the man was committing trespassing by walking on someone else's property. The case was eventually settled, but it was a nasty episode, and it did the insurance company little good when the tiff went public.

"Meaning that any illegal activity could be grounds to deny the claim," I said.

"It's possible," Harold shrugged. "Let's just say we'd prefer everyone lead a long, safe life. Works out best for all of us."

"Okay. Tell me about Curtis's wife. How long have they

been married?"

"Couple of years. Second marriage," he said.

"He trade up for a newer model?" I asked.

Harold shook his head. "Not exactly. Sad story, actually. His first wife passed away. Heart issues. Doctors have made a lot of advances, but I guess they caught it too late. Curtis had been married for almost 25 years. Quite a shock. Maybe not so shocking was the fact that he got married a year after his first wife passed."

I nodded. Some men did not operate well as bachelors, and simply preferred to be married. "You knew Curtis well over the years?" I asked.

"He's been a client of Differential since he got married. So we became acquainted. We have a few friends in common. But when he asked for those ten million dollar policies, I did a thorough background check on both of them. Nothing registered as unusual. No red flags to speak of."

"That was then, this is now."

"Yup."

"And what changed was he now has a new wife," I said, using my finely honed detective skills. "My guess is she's a lot different from his first. Tell me about her."

Harold put his fork down and signaled to the waiter for more coffee, his cup being three-quarters empty. After it was refilled, he poured in a little cream, then a little more cream, then dug into the small sugar bowl and pulled out a carefully measured dose and stirred it in. Taking a sip, he looked down and frowned at it.

"I can never get the mixture quite right after the first cup," he sighed. "I swear it takes a chemist to know how to get the proper balance again."

"That's why I learned to drink it black," I shrugged, thinking back to my many diner breakfasts as a cop, when the overly helpful waitress would slosh more coffee into the cup whether I asked for it or not. Taking it black solved the problem of recreating the right blend of cream and sugar.

"Lauren is from Wyoming. Lauren Crum, or I guess Lauren Starr now. Father's a cowboy, mother's a barmaid, you can probably figure out her upbringing. Beautiful girl, though, a former Miss Teen USA. That got her out of Wyoming. Otherwise, she's just another blonde cowgirl, spending her time flirting with ranch hands until one gets her pregnant. But I guess she had some other talent, had a big voice. Couple that with winning a beauty pageant and that got some attention in Tinseltown. An agent found her a singing gig out here, told her she'd be able to make her own album. That was her big dream, so she up and moved to L.A. She's doing okay. The album sold well, and she's toured with some big names."

"Dreams sometimes come true," I said, taking a final bite of hash. "At least for a little while. How old is she now?"

"She is 25. Oh, and she's also a twin. Identical sister named Jacquie."

"Lauren and Jacquie. I would assume Jacquie finished second in the contest?"

"Er, not so much," he said. "Car accident at fourteen."

"Ouch."

"Yeah. Made the mistake of sitting in the front seat without a seat belt. My guess is they don't have great plastic surgeons in Wyoming. But she helps Lauren out. Not exactly a personal assistant, not exactly a business manager."

"Uh-huh," I said. "So, Lauren escapes the hardscrabble life in the prairie, which has to be quite different from Los Angeles. And I doubt there were a lot of rich men like Curtis Starr around. Small-town beauty meets millionaire former athlete. Sounds like a romance novel. Any trouble brewing between her and Brady? Or with her and Curtis?"

"I don't know. Maybe both. She thinks Curtis should be more supportive of her music career. He thinks Lauren needs to be around more for him. Brady's actually talked to me about it. Not a problem when he's down in San Diego for school, but when he's home, there's tension. Maybe it has something to do with the fact that Lauren is only three years older than her new stepson."

"Okay. And what is it you'd like from me. I mean, aside from saving the Differential from having to pay out ten or twenty million bucks if Curtis Starr or his wife somehow become the victims of an accident. Or something sinister."

Harold considered this as he scooped up another forkful of eggs Benedict. "That's the big picture goal. Figuring out how to get there is what I'm hiring you to do. And paying your daily rate, which is not insignificant, if I recall."

"It is not," I smiled. "And there may be some extra expenses involved."

"We have some discretionary funds set aside. And it's still April, which means the bean counters in Finance haven't cut my budget yet."

"Good to know. I'll poke around. Would be nice if you could give Curtis a heads up I'm coming there. Although how you do that and not raise eyebrows will be tricky."

"I don't know if I can do that," Harold sighed. "Curtis has an independent streak. It might be best just to stay inconspicuous."

"Fine," I said, finishing the rest of my hash and washing it down with a big gulp of coffee. I decided the food was good but I was mostly paying for atmosphere. "I'm curious about something. How did Curtis and Lauren meet?"

"Mutual friend. I think you know him, too. He's Brady's agent. Name's Cliff Roper. Does that ring a bell?"

I sighed and stared at my empty plate. Cliff Roper. Yes, I did know him. I certainly did

To read the rest of Hard Count, please purchase it on

Amazon.com

Thank you!

Swim Move

www.ingramcontent.com/pod-product-compliance
Lightning Source LLC
Chambersburg PA
CBHW020826260626
47169CB00003B/848